Peirene

CLAUDIO MORANDINI

TRANSLATED FROM THE ITALIAN
BY J OCKENDEN

Neve, cane, piede

AUTHOR

Claudio Morandini lives in Aosta, where he balances his career as a writer with his work as a teacher. *Neve, cane, piede*, first published in 2015, has been a literary phenomenon: a top-five Italian bestseller, the novel won the Procida – Isola di Arturo – Elsa Morante Prize in 2016 and has been translated into French, Spanish and Turkish. It appears here for the first time in English.

TRANSLATOR

J Ockenden is a translator, journalist, broadcaster, poet and winner of the 2019 Peirene Stevns Translation Prize. After entering the prize with an impeccable translation of the first chapter of *Snow, Dog, Foot*, J was awarded a writer's retreat in the Pyrenees, where the work was completed. This is J's first full-length literary translation.

MEIKE ZIERVOGEL
PEIRENE PRESS

This strange little book stayed with me. Images slipped from the pages and lodged themselves in my mind: the beautiful but hostile mountain, the isolated cabin, the grumpy old man who refuses to be helped and the stray dog in need of a friend. It is a book full of humour, grit and empathy that made me laugh and cry in equal measure.

First published in Great Britain in 2019 by
Peirene Press Ltd
17 Cheverton Road
London N19 3BB
www.peirenepress.com

First published under the original Italian-language title *Neve, cane, piede*
by Exòrma Edizioni, Rome, Italy

With special thanks to Gesche Ipsen, who edited *Snow, Dog, Foot* for
Peirene Press, and to Jennifer Higgins, who offered editorial support
as part of the Peirene Stevns Translation Prize mentorship.

ISBN 978-1-908670-56-4

Designed by Sacha Davison Lunt
Cover image: Alastair Wallace / Shutterstock
Typeset by Tetragon, London
Printed and bound by CPI Group (UK) Ltd, Croydon, CR0 4YY

The translation of this work was supported by the Peirene Stevns Translation Prize,
which was established with the generous support of Martha Stevns in 2018.

CLAUDIO MORANDINI

TRANSLATED FROM THE ITALIAN
BY J OCKENDEN

Peirene

Snow, Dog, Foot

1

The first signs of the approaching autumn send Adelmo Farandola down to the village to fetch supplies. Leaving his cabin in the morning, he sees that the grass in the surrounding meadows is rimed with frost that stubbornly refuses to melt. Relentless icy winds blow through the valley and slip between cracks in the cabin walls, seeming to hammer on the door day and night. The clouds swell and bear down oppressively, no longer distinguishable from the valley's rock walls.

Down to the village, then, before it's too late and a sudden fall of snow makes the path treacherous. Adelmo Farandola walks, his rucksack on his back. He needs dried meat, dried sausages, wine and butter. The potatoes he has put aside will see him through the whole winter. They're lying in the stable now, in the dark, next to some old farm tools: wooden pails, bridles, butter churns, chains and brushes. They reach out with their pale sprouts as though to tickle someone. There are plenty of potatoes – and apples too, crates of apples, which the cold weather will sour but leave edible. Adelmo Farandola loves the taste of those ugly apples, a taste that coats his teeth and clings to the hairs lining his nostrils, an almost meaty taste, like well-hung game left over after a successful hunt. There are apples too, enough for winter. He still needs sausages, and wine. Wine and butter. Butter and salt.

He is bent double by a crosswind as he makes his way down to the village. The going is surprisingly difficult and he almost laughs thinking how he will struggle on the return, coming back uphill in this wind. The path slithers down through gullies and across plateaus, occasionally losing itself between old rotting tree stumps, long grasses and the ever-shifting scree, but the man knows how to find his way.

Here, halfway down, the autumn weather has turned the larches a wan yellow. This isn't the cheerful, brazen autumn you find at the bottom of the valley, where the vineyards and forests of alder and chestnut add colour to the landscape. Here, the leaves die quickly, drying out on the branches even before they fall.

Adelmo Farandola used to go down to the village more often, to hear the band play on high days and holidays. He would lurk behind the walls of the houses and let the music reach him in a confused swirl of notes. But he soon stopped that, because someone had seen him and come up to him, hand outstretched, and tried to engage him in conversation. Now he stops when he reaches the line of beech trees and listens to the band play from there, well hidden among the leaves and trunks. The music rises up indistinctly, a mess of drumbeats, tubas and shrill clarinets quavering on the breeze, but that's enough for him. From time to time he finds himself recognizing some tune or other and even feels moved to sing it to himself – and so he does, but very quietly, because he doesn't want to be overheard by anyone wandering nearby, ready to come up to him and shake his hand and not let go and ask him about things that he doesn't know or doesn't remember, doesn't care about or doesn't want to talk about.

After a few minutes, however, even the band makes him feel nauseous. There are too many people, he thinks, too tightly packed, too noisy, too cheerful. So he spits on the ground, turns away and starts back homewards up the steep slope, telling himself that the band really does play badly, that the villagers are all stupid and that music is useless anyway.

But sometimes he dreams about the band, and in his dream he hears melodies of extraordinary beauty performed by musicians playing perfectly in tune. Fearlessly, he joins them, following behind and singing along in full voice with the music, which would perhaps bring back distant memories of his youth, if he had managed to keep those memories intact. Memories of dancing with girls and, in particular, scrapping and fighting with other suitors, and of long conversations with girls, consisting mostly of silences and sighs and drunken hiccups.

A vague feeling steals over Adelmo Farandola as he reaches the first houses of the village. He looks around and everything seems less strange than it usually does when he comes to stock up after months of solitude on the mountain. He starts confidently down the main street (the only one you could call a street) and finds his way to the shop (the only one worthy of the name) with astonishing ease. The shop faces out onto the square in front of the church (the only square you could call a square) and its window is cluttered with dusty tools and gifts that have become almost colourless from long exposure to the sun. They sell all sorts of things here: food and farming tools, linen and newspapers, even a few trinkets for ladies.

Adelmo Farandola enters, automatically bowing his head at the door – as people do in reverence when they go into church, or as he always does to avoid smacking his head on the low lintel of his cabin. The lady behind the counter looks at him in surprise and smiles.

'Good morning,' she says. 'Leave the door open, thanks.'

'Good morning,' Adelmo Farandola replies slowly. It's been so long since he's spoken to anyone that he struggles to get the words out, and each one feels as difficult as a tongue-twister. In his confusion, he shuts the door behind him.

'Forgotten something?'

'No, I… I need to get things.'

'That's what I mean. Things you forgot last time.'

'Last time,' he murmurs.

'Yes, last week. When was it, Tuesday? Wednesday? Perhaps you remember.'

'I… I've come to get supplies.'

'Yes, I can see that. But since you came by last week with that same face on to stock up for the winter, I'm wondering whether perhaps you forgot something, and if so, what you could have forgotten last time that's so terribly important, since it's not exactly a walk in the park getting down here and then going all the way back up to… wherever it is that you go – I've actually never really understood where that is.'

The lady's tongue is well versed in conversation. Adelmo Farandola, meanwhile, accustomed to months of silence, is as incapable of listening as he is of expressing himself.

'And given that last time – on Tuesday or Wednesday last week – you loaded yourself up with a fair bit of stuff, I was wondering what on earth you could have forgotten. Or did you come by just to see me?' The lady laughs, a nice long cackle that makes poor Adelmo Farandola tremble and long to flee the shop without buying anything.

Instead he makes a colossal effort and stammers, 'I... I haven't come down since last April –'

'But I'm telling you, I saw you here! On Tuesday or Wednesday! Are you teasing me?'

'No, I...'

Another customer enters, an old man from the village who used to repair tools. The jingle of the bell makes Adelmo Farandola jump and take a step backwards into a dark corner.

The old man sniffs the air and laughs.

'Something the matter?' he asks the lady.

'Benito!' she calls to the new arrival, laughing. 'Mr Adelmo here is having me on. He's pretending he doesn't remember coming by last week and cleaning out my shop for the winter. Leave the door open, thanks.'

The old man laughs again and passes a finger over his grey moustache, saying nothing.

'I... I haven't come down since April,' Adelmo Farandola stammers again.

The old man laughs but doesn't say anything.

'Benito, you tell Mr Adelmo that he was here on Tuesday or Wednesday and ransacked my whole shop.'

'Mm, that's right. I saw you too,' the old man laughs.

'But where?'

'Right out there, in the street. All loaded up like a mule.'

'There, what did I say?' the woman concludes triumphantly. 'But Mr Adelmo always has to have his little joke, pretending not to remember.'

It's Adelmo Farandola's turn to say nothing. He never jokes. He doesn't know how. He doesn't even know what joking is and, if it ever occurred to him to make a joke, no one would realize because he doesn't know how and, if anything, they would take him for an idiot, which is what is happening now.

'So, what would you like?' asks the lady, her manner more brisk now that she has another customer waiting.

'Well, I... I...'

'Yes, you...'

'I don't remember exactly what I got last time.'

'What do you mean you don't remember?'

The old man laughs to himself, amused by this forgetful mountain dweller.

'I don't remember what I bought... but I need some salt –'

'But I've already given you three bags!'

'And butter –'

'Three kilos! What exactly are you going to do with all that butter?'

'And wine –'

'Ah, you can never have enough of that,' laughs the old man.

'Five litres wasn't enough for you? When I saw you leave carrying all that stuff, I thought you'd never make it back up! How did you manage it, anyway?' Then, with a wink: 'Don't tell me you've already polished off the lot!'

The old man laughs and laughs.

'Wine always runs out too soon!' he laughs.

Enough. In the end, to avoid leaving empty-handed, Adelmo Farandola buys two bottles of red wine and three pairs of woollen knee socks. He pays with large, grimy, crumpled banknotes, which the lady accepts with a sigh, and goes out into the already wintry wind.

'Leave the door open,' the lady shouts after him.

A memory, albeit a rather vague one, has begun to coalesce in his mind. These houses and these stones really do seem more familiar than they ought to. He has been to the shop recently, he has already bought supplies – the lady was right. He begins to remember climbing back up to his valley, weighed down by the five-litre bottle and his other purchases. He remembers the sweat, the pain in his arms and back, and the sound of his own ragged breathing, which he, in his confusion, thought was coming from someone beside him, so that he stopped more than once to ask, 'Who's there?' Or is that just the memory of the other times he's followed the same path, weighed down by the same things, in previous years? He shakes his head slowly as he starts up the road leading out of the village, which narrows to a cart track that winds between fields and vegetable patches, full of the stink of food scraps and rows of rotting cabbages, before shrinking down to a footpath, which grows steep as it reaches the first larches and starts climbing towards the Alpine pastures above.

2

Adelmo Farandola makes his way back up, confused and despondent. He doesn't remember – he doesn't remember having forgotten. From time to time a nagging feeling returns: the feeling of having been the butt of a joke between the idiotic old man and the lady in the shop. 'They sit there, waiting for me to come down, just so they can make a fool of me. These village types,' he says, and spits on the ground. He says it in the same way that people from the village say 'these city types', spitting on the ground in the same way.

'I'll look in the stable once I get back to my pasture. First thing, I'll look in the stable. That's where I always put the stuff I buy down there. In the stable, where it's cool and everything keeps for months. As soon as I get back, I'll check. And if I don't find anything I'll go back down there and give them a piece of my mind.'

With each step, Adelmo Farandola plots his revenge. He runs through the options: burning down the lady's shop, ambushing the old man, giving both of them a good hiding. Ruminating on vengeance gives him a bit of peace, offers him a modicum of satisfaction. It's not the same as doing it for real, but it's close enough, especially since after years of solitude true things become indistinguishable from dreams. At the end of one daydream – a daydream in which the whole village is consumed by flames, high, roaring flames against which shadowy firefighters struggle in vain, above which the blades of water-bearing helicopters beat in vain – Adelmo Farandola, mollified, sits down on a boulder and even manages a smile. He'll look in the stable, definitely, first thing. But that earlier, needling feeling of having been the victim of a practical joke has gone. He'll look in the stable, because you never know. Now the imaginary flames have finally been extinguished and he pictures himself peering into the open stable through a haze of smoke, glimpsing food and wine inside.

In the middle of the larch copse, right where the path begins to climb without even a curve or two to relieve the steepness, Adelmo Farandola hears a sound like heavy breathing behind him. 'Who's there?' he asks, wheezing a little from tiredness.

No one answers, but the panting doesn't stop.

'Who's there?'

Eventually, a dog pokes its head out from behind a teeming anthill: an old dog of no particular breed, its tongue lolling, its ears down, and its eyes – each of them a different colour – open wide.

The man bends down to pick up a stone and throws it. The dog doesn't even flinch, letting the stone hit its neck with barely a whine.

'Go on, shoo!' Adelmo Farandola shouts, and starts walking again.

The dog continues to trail him, with its head lowered. It looks like it's starving. Adelmo Farandola lets it follow for a bit, feigning indifference. He even tries to whistle, although he doesn't know how and just hisses tunelessly between his teeth.

He is almost surprised to see the rock walls that surround the pasture in front of him. Without thinking, he's been tracing a familiar route, step by step, and suddenly he's arrived.

'The pasture,' he mutters to himself, with an astonishment that makes the dog whine.

Adelmo Farandola glances at it and it yelps again inquisitively. The man would like to say something to it, but he doesn't know what to say to a dog so he keeps quiet. Maybe later I'll whistle to it, he thinks. Dogs like the sound of whistling. Later I'll whistle to it a bit and we'll see how it reacts. The dog's long tongue is hanging out from thirst and tiredness, and it launches itself at a puddle of putrid water at the edge of the path and starts lapping at it. Adelmo Farandola lets it. He's thirsty too, come to that.

The feeling of dryness in his throat suddenly reminds him of the wine. He walks towards the stable, the cold, dark stable that once contained some cows which have long since disappeared.

'Who knows what happened to those cows?' he says. 'Perhaps they're dead. More likely someone came and stole them. You let yourself get distracted and *they* – they come and steal your cows from right under your nose. And it's not just me it happens to. They're always stealing animals from us poor folk.'

He goes to the stable and opens the door. The five-litre bottle of wine is there, in the dark, next to a broken butter churn. There are the crates of apples too, smelling like dried meat, and the boxes of potatoes, their pale roots reaching out like little legs. There's the jerrycan of alcohol. There are the dried sausages, hanging from a beam. He can just make out a few loaves on top of the dusty bread bin, which have dried out and become infested with flour moths. There's all the firewood collected over the summer. The bottles of milk are there. The butter. It's all there.

The smell of fermenting apples makes the dog sneeze. It wants to come in and sniff around. Adelmo Farandola tells it no. It's the first word he addresses to the dog: 'No.' To underline the point, he gives its flank a kick. The dog understands and retreats with its head bowed. It makes do with the slight feeling of drunkenness that animals get from the smell of fermenting food.

For the rest of that day Adelmo Farandola allows the dog to tag along after him, partly out of apathy and partly out of pity, letting it stick its nose inside the cabin, into the big room where he eats and sleeps and passes the time. He even goes so far as to call it to him, as it lingers shyly on the threshold with its ears down.

'What are you doing there?' asks the man. 'Come in. Shut the door,' he says. 'You'll let the cold in.'

The dog advances cautiously. After a couple of minutes, Adelmo Farandola goes to shut the door. Then he sits down by the stove and waits for the strength to light it. The cabin is cold: filled with a damp, static cold that chills him to the bone and traces painful circles around his eyes. As he sits, Adelmo Farandola shuts his eyes, sighs, lets his heavy head fall and nods off.

When he wakes up, the dog is still there, lying at his feet – if anything, a little closer than before. It gazes at him with its head on its paws and its ears pricked up. The man yawns, burps, farts and burps again, and the dog's ears briefly twitch at each noise. It's time to light the stove, Adelmo Farandola says to himself. It's dark. Time to light it.

The fire takes a while to crackle into life in the blackened stove, but it gets going eventually, fed with paper from damp old magazines and twigs and alcohol, and the flames spread. It doesn't give much light and at first seems merely to hint at the possibility of heat. It is only after half an hour, once night has fallen outside and the cold has become unbearable, that the first vague traces of heat begin to curl out of the stove.

'Do you like that?' Adelmo Farandola asks, after a while. He finds talking to himself quite natural, but talking to a dog makes him uncomfortable. 'Do you like that?' he asks, making an effort. If this animal's going to stick around, he might as well start practising straight away. Who knows, he muses, perhaps it's a farm dog. 'Are you a farm dog?'

The dog sits up, waiting for something.

'Are you a sheepdog?'

The dog whines.

'That would be handy for the cows,' says Adelmo Farandola, before remembering that it's been years since he had any cows and that the stable, with its floor covered in old stamped-down manure, is cold and empty.

'Never mind,' he says. 'Can you keep watch? Can you bite troublemakers?'

The dog barks. The man decides to take this as a yes.

'Because, you see, we get a lot of them up here. That's why I move further up the mountain in the summer, where they can't reach me. This summer, for example…'

He stops to feed the fire.

'…this summer, three idiots arrived with rucksacks. They kept talking to me, on and on and on like you wouldn't believe. "I've got nothing. I've got nothing!" I told them. They didn't believe me. They wanted to come into my house. They wanted to steal my cheese. "I haven't got any cheese!" I told them. They wanted to take pictures of me. They wanted to laugh at me when they got home, I'm sure of it. "I don't want to. I don't like photographs!" I said. But they just carried on regardless. I had to throw stones at them. Luckily there's no shortage of stones here. There are more stones than there are blades of grass. I threw hundreds of stones at them, hundreds! I think I even hit them. They ran away down the path, the idiots. I saw them fall over.'

The man sniggers.

'Now you,' he says to the dog, 'would you have been able to take a good bite out of them? Then you'd be useful to me. If not, I could keep you anyway. No, not for company. I don't need company. But in case the provisions run out sooner than expected.'

The dog is hanging on his every word.

'There are countries where they eat dogs all the time. I don't see anything wrong with it. You're animals, after all, like the rest. Meat. It's fine as long as you cook it right.'

The fire is crackling now.

'I don't see anything wrong with it,' Adelmo Farandola repeats, after a brief yelp from the dog.

The next morning, Adelmo Farandola and the dog go out to get some fresh air and piss against one of the many heaps of stones.

The pasture lies in a hollow whose grassy floor is dotted with these heaps, piled up by shepherds over the centuries as they cleared sections of meadowland. But scree and pebbles kept falling from above, shaken loose by constant landslides and subsidence, covering the plots cleared by the shepherds, burying them under still more stones. For generations, men tried to salvage a few plants and grasses in this unfriendly hollow, a few buttercups and snowbells, primroses and Alpine anemones, clover and cereal for their few cows. These were generations made obstinate by poverty and the narrowness of their horizons. It was only in the last century that they realized it was more productive to give up on the rocky valley altogether and migrate somewhere less landslide-prone, leaving the hollow to fill up with detritus and rock fragments like a dry riverbed. Now it's inhabited by a mute assembly of stone idols, vaguely human-shaped cones and hemispheres sitting on the eternally crushed grass, seeming to keep a watchful eye on the rare passers-by.

When the sun comes up, Adelmo Farandola calls the dog and invites it to join him in the sunshine.

During the warmest days of autumn, the little scraps of meadow that survive in between the piled-up stones are full of frenzied grasshoppers that jump madly, blindly, in all directions at the slightest hint of danger. When they hear the man and the dog approaching, the grasshoppers become so desperate to escape that they land on them in clouds, jumping into their eyes and into their mouths. Adelmo Farandola and the dog rather enjoy this frenzy and they open their jaws wide to let the insects hurl themselves inside. The dog gives them a quick chew, just for a laugh, before spitting out the clump of wings and little legs that it doesn't want to eat. Adelmo Farandola chews more methodically and, more often than not, opts to swallow.

Between the borage leaves and clumps of saxifrage, countless spiders spin fibrous webs, enveloping the blades of grass in whitish coils until they are almost completely hidden.

The dog examines these minute beings.

'Go on!' the man encourages it cheerfully. 'Taste them! Taste them!'

3

The dog ends up sticking around, day after day. When night falls, Adelmo Farandola leaves it outside, where it howls for hours before resigning itself to sleeping curled up on the old blanket the man has left out for it. Sometimes, in the night, he hears it barking at some animal or other – a weasel or a hare. It barks itself hoarse, but doesn't abandon the house to run after its quarry. It hasn't taken long for the dog to realize that it's unwise to go chasing after much faster animals, risking its life running across the rocky crags and getting a hoof in the face for its trouble. Instead, it waits for the man to throw it a few scraps from his dinner.

He's a good dog, in his way; or perhaps he's just old and has lost his illusions along with his youth and strength. Sometimes, to reward him for being so pliant, the man lets him into the house, where he sniffs everything avidly. Adelmo Farandola lost his sense of smell some time ago. When he stopped washing, he became immune to his own odours, and the farts he expels under the blankets at night feel like warm caresses. He is careful to encourage them with a suitable diet. He is amazed to see the dog sniffing everything – it had never occurred to him that there were so many smells around. The dog sniffs him too, paying particular attention to his shoes and ankles, grateful for these odours that seem to sustain him like morsels of food.

One day Adelmo Farandola catches himself talking to the dog. 'Do this, do that,' he says. He tells him things, here and there. He asks the dog whether he's seen a thing that he can't just this moment lay his hand on in the cabin. He tells him about the snow that will pile up outside all winter long, until they won't be able to see a thing because everything will be snow, and about how they'll be buried inside and the roof, weighed down with snow, will threaten to collapse at any moment.

He says it to see how the dog reacts, to see if he gets scared.

The dog pricks up his ears and sticks out his red tongue, his eyes bright. If he had a tail, he would wag it, like all dogs with tails do. Adelmo Farandola offers him a bite of food and says, 'Good, isn't it?' or 'Last year's bread was better.'

The dog shakes his head and takes a deep breath, as though he's about to say something in reply.

'Last year the bread was nice and sweet,' the man says, 'nice and sweet. You take a piece and you dip it in the wine. Like this.'

He demonstrates. The dog watches his every movement.

'Then you take it out and do this.'

Adelmo Farandola shoves the bit of wine-soaked bread into his mouth with dripping fingers. A delicate, distant flavour floods his mouth. If he hadn't stopped brushing his teeth years ago, the taste would be strong, pungent and invasive, but now it slips quickly and faintly past his last few encrusted teeth and across his white-coated tongue.

'Mmm, that's good,' he says with pleasure, looking straight into the shining eyes of the dog sitting in front of him. 'That's good.'

The dog's tongue drips like a leaky tap and his drool creates a spreading puddle on the floor.

At the second wine-soaked morsel, he begins to swallow mouthfuls of air.

'Can I try a bit?' he asks the man at last.

'No,' says Adelmo Farandola, who is just getting started on his third piece.

'Just a little bit,' says the dog. 'Please. Just a teeny little bit.'

'No.'

'Just to see what it's like. How do I know you're telling the truth unless I taste it?'

'You take it on trust.'

'I'd rather try for myself.'

The third bite is gone. The man is beginning to feel satisfied. He doesn't fill his stomach these days; he knows how to stop himself almost immediately. The need for rationing in winter and the long walk to the village have trained him to be content with very little – almost nothing, in fact. His stomach's rumblings have transformed into a kind of internal voice, which he talks to sometimes, about this and that.

But now there's the dog to talk to.

'Where were we?' prompts the dog.

To shut him up, Adelmo Farandola throws him a chunk of dry bread. With a snort that might be a sigh of relief, the dog jumps for the morsel and snaps it up at once. Then he turns back to the man as if nothing had happened.

'Is there anything else for me?' he asks.

'You've just had your dinner!'

'A piece of dry bread! Do you want me to die right here in front of you? I need real nourishment. I can't eat imaginary food. A little scrap like that isn't enough.'

'You're not having my wine.'

'Never mind about the wine. I was thinking more of a bit of sausage.'

'Were you now?'

'Dogs are carnivores! We can't live on dry bread. We're not chickens – no offence to chickens.'

For a moment, the dog opens his jaws and hungrily chews on the air. Perhaps the reference to chickens has reminded him how much he likes raw meat, torn from a still-living animal. How good it feels to plunge your muzzle into your living prey, into a mess of ruffled feathers and struggling legs.

'What was I saying?' he asks, composing himself.

'You were talking about sausages,' says Adelmo Farandola, 'but you can forget it.'

The dog's muzzle turns out to be covered in yellow blisters. Between the tufts of his bristly fur, numerous ticks lie blissfully burrowed under the skin, their stomachs swelling with blood.

'You're covered in ticks!' Adelmo Farandola shouts, when he notices them.

'Ticks?' the dog asks. 'Where? Where?' He turns in circles, trying to bite the tail he doesn't have.

'Everywhere, you filthy creature! On your head, behind your ears, on your muzzle, on your neck, on your stomach, on your paws!' the man exclaims, exploring the dog's fur, rolling it over and feeling it. 'Stay still while I look at you.'

The dog whines affectionately at his touch.

'Stop that. I'm not cuddling you.'

'You're not?'

'No, I'm looking for ticks.'

'Ticks? Where, where, where?' Laughing happily, the dog starts chasing his non-existent tail again, just for the pleasure of exasperating the man.

'You don't get ticks up here in the mountains,' Adelmo Farandola pronounces after his examination. 'You get them further down, in the meadows, in the long grass down in the valley.'

'Oh, well then, I must have picked them up there. But I can't feel them. Trust me, they don't bother me at all. Who knows how long I've been carrying them around.'

'They're sucking your blood, idiot.'

'Really?'

'I'll have to burn them off you.'

'You're joking, right?'

Adelmo Farandola opens the stove and, using a pair of tongs, pulls out a red-hot ember and moves it towards the dog's face.

'Don't even think about it!' the dog barks, running away.

'Come here. It's the ticks I'm burning, not you.'

'Get knotted! I'm not letting you set fire to me!'

They chase each other for a long time, round and round the cabin's one room, until the ember turns black and Adelmo Farandola runs out of breath.

The man waits until the dog falls asleep and starts to snore. Then he extracts another ember, creeps stealthily towards the animal, grabs him and touches the burning ember to his neck. The dog wakes up, barks, screams and struggles, but Adelmo Farandola manages to burn two or three ticks before letting him wriggle free.

'Are you mad?' the dog barks indignantly.

'I'll do that every time you fall asleep,' says Adelmo Farandola. 'I just have to wait. It'll be a long winter and I don't have much else to do.'

'Don't ever do that again, friend,' barks the dog.

'You're free to leave. You choose.'

The dog huffs, snorts, sniffs. 'I'm on fire!' he cries, still shaken.

'I don't think so,' the man scoffs. 'It's just the smell of burning fur.'

'My burning fur. Mine! And burning blood too.'

'That blood was feeding the ticks.'

'Disgusting animals,' the dog says, and sneezes.

'That's the problem with you creatures,' says Adelmo Farandola. 'Always rummaging around with your muzzles to the ground, sticking your noses in the grass, rolling around in the dust and the dirt, and piles of other animals' shit –'

'Well, yes, I suppose I have been known to…'

'You get what you deserve, then.'

In the evenings, the dog tries to stay alert, but he's an elderly mutt and sooner or later sleep overtakes him. That's the moment Adelmo Farandola has been waiting for: he grabs a large ember with the tongs and sticks it in the dog's fur. There are screams, barks, sobs, sometimes even the odd bite. Then the whole thing begins again.

'I want to see which of us is more stubborn,' the man says.

But all this rummaging around in the dog's straw-coloured fur has consequences. One day, as he gives himself a little scratch, Adelmo Farandola notices a tick on his right forearm. He looks closer. There's another one, and another, practically under his armpit. One more on the other arm, two more above the ankles.

The dog laughs, thinking how much he will enjoy watching the man burn his own ticks off with an ember, smelling the burning blood again.

'You've given me a little present,' says Adelmo Farandola.

'I hope you like it,' the dog replies, with rare sarcasm.

Adelmo Farandola hasn't washed in months, letting his stench create a cloud of warmth around him. Sweat and grime have been allowed to build up on his skin in peace, alongside wind-blown dirt, dust from the stable, the various pollens that colour the air at certain times of year, and clumps of dead skin. With the passing months he has developed a delightful sticky coating all over his body, which he only notices from time to time when a little itch awakens him from a daze and obliges him to bend and contort himself to reach the spot he needs to scratch. His skin has turned brown, the colour of sun-baked dust and mud.

What does it matter if people keep their distance from him or fling open doors and windows when he passes, or cover their mouths with their hands to avoid breathing in? Actually, it's better this way. You can't trust people who wash and live cleanly and change their sheets and wash and air their linen, who primp and perfume themselves, who want to seem more beautiful than they are, who pretend not to stink. They're the ones who get ill at the drop of a hat, from a tiny draught from a window, from someone sneezing in their face, from a moment of inattention. They die for no good reason, weakened by all that water, dazed by all that perfume.

Adelmo Farandola hasn't undressed in years. He hasn't brushed his teeth in years, because you need to look after your teeth and not go weakening them with brushing. For years he hasn't cleaned himself after urinating or defecating because it's not good to get too interested in those parts, and it's certainly not healthy to go fiddling around among those organs that deal with the voiding of the stomach. He cultivates a patina of sweat which flourishes in the forest of his armpit hair and encircles his ribcage. For years, he's allowed his feet (which he has recently swathed in three pairs of woollen knee socks, layered one on top of the other and never changed) to boil inside his boots, the blackened nails curling until they eventually break off by themselves. For years, he has cultivated and encouraged the patches of crusty skin that appear between the greasy and increasingly sparse hairs of his head, his beard and his unkempt eyebrows.

This, he firmly believes, is the best way to face the winter. This coat of grime must be protected from the weather (above all from the rain that threatens to wash him and expose his bare skin to illnesses) and from the dog's affectionate licking. This extra layer of protection accompanies him like a second skin.

4

Adelmo Farandola knows that there's been a mountain ranger keeping an eye on him for some time now. He noticed that he was being watched from afar by a man in uniform, holding a pair of binoculars up to his eyes. Adelmo Farandola also has an old pair of binoculars, so one day he picked them up and started watching the man who was watching him. There he was: a ranger, with his rifle on his back. He stood alone, quite still, his binoculars trained on the cabin. He'd already begun hovering around the pasture in late summer, long before the snow came down and covered everything. Then, after the first snowfall, he climbed up as far as the steep ridge marking out the lower part of the valley and stopped there to have a look around.

But Adelmo Farandola is sure that he had felt the ranger watching him even earlier than that, back in midsummer, when he was in his summer shelter hidden among the avalanche debris further up the mountain. He no longer needs to see him – he knows now that the ranger has him under observation. Adelmo Farandola climbs to the mouth of the furthest gully, leading up to the shelter, and watches. He watches and waits for the ranger to approach him. He could throw stones at him from up here. He could cause a landslide and bury him beneath several tons of rubble. It wouldn't be difficult – rocks are always shifting up here. Put one foot wrong and you could find yourself plummeting into the valley below with half a mountain on top of you. He hesitates to do it, though, because this man wears a uniform and hurting him might lead to trouble.

Sometimes the ranger seems emboldened and approaches without bothering to hide himself. He pretends that he just happened to be in the neighbourhood of the cabin or the shelter, and looks around as though his mind is on other things – the animals scampering over the rocks, the flight of vultures overhead or the colonies of marmots further up the mountain. But Adelmo Farandola knows that the ranger is looking his way, out of the corner of his eye.

He has nothing to hide, this man who talks to himself. The pasture is his. The clearing is his. The whole valley is his. He can do what he wants with it. The animals are his, just like the rocks and the grass and the water and the ice. And if now and again he shoots a chamois for his dinner, he isn't accountable to anyone for it. The chamois are his: their flesh and bones, horns and hides, flesh, bones and horns all belong to him. He bought the valley and its land years ago with his brother, using the money from the sale of the other valley, the nicer one, the one where the big developer from the city put up factories and hotels. He doesn't care about that other valley any more. It's been abandoned by animals and mountain people, and now it coughs up flashes of light and discordant snatches of voices and music and engines, and curls of smoke. Here, he is in charge, in this valley that no one cares about because it's ugly and rocky and doesn't lead anywhere, and is too steep and fills up with debris in winter, and is mangled by raging torrents in spring and autumn. He doesn't want anything more; he doesn't ask for anything more. So that bloody ranger can go and do one.

'Good morning!' the ranger calls to him one day.

Adelmo Farandola starts, but pretends he hasn't heard and doesn't reply. The dog barks in surprise and hides behind the old man's legs with a growl.

'Good morning,' the ranger repeats, closer now. 'Lovely day, isn't it?'

A grunt, nothing more.

'Nice to see you again! How are you?'

Grunt, shrug. Why is he talking about seeing me again, Adelmo Farandola wonders, when this is the first time we've spoken?

'I get it, you know,' says the ranger, reaching out to stroke the dog. 'Good dog, good dog. I mean, I get why you live up here. I like wild places too, the places no one else likes, the bits they leave blank on tourist maps. Like this valley. I think it's magnificent. Look how much life there is! Look!'

The ranger waves his arm, pointing out what Adelmo Farandola already knows: all around them the rocks teem with an excitable, unnerving throng of animals – predators and prey, the twitchy birds who are afraid of everything, but especially the skinny, dusty mammals.

'It's spectacular,' the ranger continues, 'life constantly renewing itself. The miracle of life, as they say. I understand you and I envy you, you know. But of course you do. How many times have we had this same conversation?'

Adelmo Farandola doesn't say anything, because he doesn't remember ever having had this conversation, but he doesn't leave because he doesn't want the ranger to follow him. Above all, he doesn't want the ranger to follow him into the cabin and stick his nose in the stable, where the chamois meat is drying and the hides, which he's planning to find a use for, are hanging from the cows' chains.

'Ah, what a life! I love this job. It makes me feel as though I'm right in the heart of God's creation, if that makes sense. It makes me feel useful. You know what I mean? Useful in some way, or at least not entirely useless. I make sure that these creatures survive. I make sure no one picks on them – or rather that no one picks them off! You understand, don't you? My colleagues are always asking me, "Why climb all the way up there? What do you think you're going to find? There's only that old hermit. You won't find anything else, not even a shrew." But I know it's not like that. The nice grassy meadows are already protected, while the unattractive valleys like this one hide the real treasures. Or rather, the real treasures hide here, if that makes sense.'

Adelmo Farandola nods wearily, to show that he has been paying attention.

'I see you agree with me, my friend.'

By the evening, Adelmo Farandola's memories of the encounter are already fuzzy. But once inside the stable he knows that he must hide the meat that he's put out to dry, and the hides, and the fleshless skulls that he might sell or get someone to sell for him next summer. He covers the hides with straw and buries the meat after wrapping it in pages from the old magazines that he normally uses to light the stove or, more rarely, to wipe his backside. He buries the skulls as well. In his head, his own voice warns him: Best to be on guard. Best to wait for a better moment.

The dog follows him without saying anything. You can tell that he's thinking about the ranger too, and perhaps he's also feeling guilty, for reasons of his own.

The next day, the young ranger shows up again.

'Good morning!' he calls from a way off.

'Good morning!' he says once he's closer.

'Good morning to you both,' he repeats when he's a foot away from Adelmo Farandola, holding out a hand, which the old man looks at but doesn't shake in the end. The dog has gone back to hiding behind his companion's legs and waits there until the intruder leaves.

'How are you today?'

Grunt.

'It's a lovely day, isn't it?'

The young man runs through his lines again. He's behaving awkwardly. He has some reason for being there that he's keeping hidden.

'What do you want?' asks Adelmo Farandola after a long moment of silence, long enough to become unbearable. That's funny, the old man thinks. I thought I was used to silence. I thought I knew how to bear it for months on end. I thought I was able to bear it for years. But now this young busybody's silence seems unbearable to me.

'Oh, I was in the area,' says the ranger. 'As I was saying yesterday, there are some lovely spots round here.'

'Yesterday?'

'That's right, yesterday. Lovely spots, full of animals.'

'Nasty creatures,' says Adelmo Farandola. Then, to the dog who's looking at him in bewilderment, he adds, 'I don't mean you.'

'What's nasty about them?'

Adelmo Farandola doesn't answer – he doesn't want to give himself away. He's afraid of letting slip that, in the stable, a few of those nasty, cautious creatures are buried under the soil and the straw.

'Do you happen to have a shotgun?' asks the ranger.

A shotgun? Adelmo Farandola thinks. What should I tell him?

'No.'

'Really?'

'No.'

'I thought you did.'

'No.'

Adelmo Farandola takes a step backwards.

'Wait, wait,' the ranger says, laughing. 'I'm not cross-examining you! I was just curious.' With a little skip, he closes the distance between them. 'Look, as far as I'm concerned, everyone should have a shotgun, especially living in these parts. You never know. It's dangerous. Anyone living alone like you do should get hold of a shotgun, if they don't have one already. Don't you think?'

'Well,' says Adelmo Farandola, staring at his feet.

'What if some wolves turn up? You know what wolves are like. What if you're attacked by a wild boar?'

'You don't get boars here. Too high up.'

'That's true. But wolves...'

'Never seen wolves.'

'Neither have I, to tell the truth. It was just a thought. But suppose something dangerous does turn up – what are you going to do, throw stones at it?'

Adelmo Farandola says nothing. He often throws stones at intruders. Sometimes he throws them blindly, to scare them off. Sometimes he focuses obstinately on the target, aiming to strike and cause pain.

'Never thrown stones.'

'Well, you've thrown stones at me a couple of times,' says the ranger, laughing again, 'but I imagine you didn't know who I was – a government official, I mean.'

'Sorry,' Adelmo Farandola forces himself to say.

'Oh, please don't worry about it. I understand, you know. I hadn't introduced myself yet. And how could I, since you kept me away with those stones? So do you have a shotgun or not?'

Adelmo Farandola hesitates.

'Well, yes,' he says at last. 'Everyone does, don't they?'

'Of course everyone does. And... you have a licence, don't you? All the documents in order?'

'Of course.'

'Ah, good man. It's important to have all the documents in order.'

'Of course.'

The ranger sighs heavily, closes his eyes and smiles at the dog.

'And could I see this licence?' he asks.

'Of course,' says Adelmo Farandola, without moving.

'Another time, perhaps,' the ranger says after a while, since nothing has happened. And off he goes, whistling.

5

At times, the dog seems like an extension of the man. He stays close to his side, rubbing up against his calf, following his every gesture, to the point where Adelmo Farandola can't get rid of him, even with a kick: whining, the dog turns in a circle a couple of times to underline the pain he feels, before returning to rub up against his friend again. Sometimes, however, an unpredictable urge sends the dog running off alone, treading lightly, nose to the ground, following traces that only he can sense. Suddenly finding himself alone, the old man calls after him, but even his shouts can't bring him back. The dog's off, he's already gone, surprisingly confident as he follows some mysterious trail, by turns straightforward and serpentine. He skirts rocks, cuts across paths and scrambles through shrubs and over tree stumps without really looking, relying solely on his nose. There – he's off, he's disappeared, he's gone. He'll stay away for hours, not returning until evening or even nightfall. Adelmo Farandola will hear the dog scratching at the door, but he won't open it – at least not straight away. Serve him right for having left him alone, for having chosen a string of bad smells over him.

*

It's funny, the man says to himself when he finds he's been abandoned. He's someone who likes solitude, that goes without saying; in fact he needs it. But he's got attached to the mongrel, and when he goes away it feels as though something inside him has died a little, and time slows down until it seems to stop altogether, and the narrow valley expands until it becomes an immense desert, and he shrinks inside this desert until he's no bigger than an ant or a worm. A mere dog can reduce him to this. God knows what effect a human being would have. Just imagine, purely hypothetically, what effect a woman would have.

'All by your lonesome today?' asks the ranger, coming up behind him on one of these occasions.

The unexpected words make him jump.

'The dog, I mean. That dog who's always by your side, where's he gone?'

'Don't know,' says Adelmo Farandola. 'Off somewhere.' After a pause he adds, 'Isn't that allowed?'

'Of course!' The ranger laughs. 'He's an animal, he needs a bit of exercise! Although...' A long pause, full of indecipherable smiles. 'Although the law does state that dogs should be kept tethered and muzzled.'

'But it's not my dog,' protests Adelmo Farandola. 'I don't know anything about it! It just started hanging around me. I don't even know its name.'

'Of course, of course.'

'I hate dogs!'

'I see. I quite understand. But you know what dogs are like. I've had dogs too, you know.'

Silence. Perhaps the ranger is waiting for Adelmo Farandola to ask about his dogs, but he stays obstinately silent.

'But anyway, next time you let him go off like that, put a muzzle on him. That way I won't be forced to shoot at him.'

'Right,' says Adelmo Farandola. Shoot at him, he thinks. Shoot at him.

'It's the law. What can you do? If I was going by the book, that dog would already be dead.'

'Of course.'

'You'll remember?'

'Remember what?'

'The muzzle. You do have one, don't you?'

'Of course,' Adelmo Farandola answers. But it's not true, he doesn't have any muzzles in the cabin. He's never had muzzles for dogs. It doesn't make sense to put a muzzle on a sheepdog – how would it do its job with its mouth clamped shut?

'Well, that's great. Now, if it's not too much trouble, I'd really love a glass of water.'

'Water?'

'Yes please. I'm so thirsty. Can we go in?'

That damned snoop, Adelmo Farandola says to himself once the ranger has finally gone away. He knows why he's here. That little pipsqueak thinks he's a poacher. He climbs all the way up here pretending to be looking for poachers, but really he has one target, just one: Farandola, Adelmo. Adelmo Farandola, who only ever fires the odd round at animals who are ill or lost. Or come to nibble at the last few blades of grass in front of the cabin. Or who climb down from the overhanging rocks, attracted by the fragrant morsels of hay that have been arranged in the yard by Adelmo Farandola, who is waiting, ready to strike as soon as they drop their guard and bow their heads to eat.

'What's wrong with that?' he asks the dog, who has finally reappeared. 'They'd die anyway, those animals. You've seen them. They're weak, they limp, they whine. I'm doing them a favour.'

'And besides,' adds the dog, 'everyone has to die sooner or later, don't they? You were saying that just the other day. But can we talk about something else?'

The dog doesn't like this topic. Last time they discussed it, Adelmo Farandola hinted that if there weren't other animals around he wouldn't think twice about killing the dog and cooking him.

'And besides, what would I do without them? I'd have no choice but to eat you,' the man says, as predicted, with a brief snigger.

'Look, that's not funny any more,' says the dog. 'And it wasn't even funny to begin with.'

'No, you're right. It's not funny.'

'Thank you.'

Adelmo Farandola doesn't have a licence. He doesn't follow rules. The valley is his. The animals are his. The air is his. Well, his and his brother's, but his brother lives a long way away and gives himself airs and wouldn't dream of setting foot in this stony valley, which they bought for a song but which he has always considered a bad deal and a waste of money. Everything here is mine, thinks Adelmo Farandola, as he lights the stove. Everything. Everything.

Since the ranger wants to treat him like a wild animal, watching him from a distance with a spyglass, Adelmo Farandola starts hiding and moving on all fours, following strange, elliptical routes that wind between the rocks and the bushes. From there, unobserved, it's his turn to spy on the ranger.

The dog follows him furtively.

'This is fun,' he says.

'Quiet! Not a sound.'

'Can't I bark?'

'No.'

'Not even a little tiny bark, just for fun?'

'No.'

The ranger approaches, then wanders off and looks around him. He seems preoccupied.

'Bloody snoop,' barks Adelmo Farandola.

'Snoop, yeah, that's right,' the dog barks as well. 'What shall we do? Shall we sneak up behind him and attack him?'

'No.'

'It would be such a good surprise. It would be really fun. I can't wait.'

Adelmo Farandola says nothing and looks surly.

6

The ranger doesn't give up. There he is, a few days later, standing like a scarecrow in the grass. The hollow is quiet, empty and dark – low clouds cover the whole valley, ready to hurl down sleet. Adelmo Farandola comes out of the cabin, slips across the meadow and hides behind some boulders abandoned on the grass millions of years earlier by a retreating glacier.

But the ranger comes straight towards him, quickly and confidently this time. Adelmo Farandola squats down and stays motionless, not even daring to breathe. The dog is behind him, flattened against the ground, his tongue hanging out in delight, his eyes shining with ancient predator memories.

'Good morning!' the ranger says, suddenly appearing next to them.

The dog explodes into a series of surprised barks.

'Good, yes, and to you,' says Adelmo Farandola.

'How's it going?'

Adelmo Farandola replies with the usual grunt.

'Looks like snow today, eh?'

'Mmm.'

'Listen, why don't you stand up? I'm finding it difficult to talk to you like this.'

The old man struggles to his feet. The dog is already sitting up, waiting for a pat.

'There we go. Now at least I can look you in the eye. I like being able to look people in the eye, don't you?'

'I don't like people.'

'Well, I'd gathered that,' says the ranger, laughing. 'And I think you're right, as always. But listen, I wanted to say –'

'I don't have a gun! Stop harassing me!'

'It's not the gun I want to talk about,' the ranger says, rather surprised. 'I'm not interested in your gun – if you have one, that is. I was thinking that, since winter is coming and living up here might start being a problem for you – living by yourself, I mean – don't you think it would be sensible to consider moving further down and staying with a friend or a relative perhaps?'

'I don't have any relatives.'

'What about your brother?'

What does he know about my brother? Adelmo Farandola thinks. Who told him that I have a brother?

'My brother is dead,' the old man lies.

'Oh, I'm sorry. I didn't know.'

'It doesn't matter.'

'When did it happen?'

'Oh, ages ago.'

'My condolences. I'm so sorry for your loss.'

'It really doesn't matter.'

The ranger pauses to reorganize his thoughts. 'But you're all right? You're really all right? Forgive me for asking, but…'

Adelmo Farandola waves his hand vaguely, as if to say that he's doing just great and hasn't a care in the world.

'...but I get the impression that you're not doing so well. In terms of health, I mean. It's cold up here. But that's not it – it's not the cold, it's the solitude. You're all alone.'

'I'm not alone,' says the old man. He looks at the dog and the dog looks back, eyes shining with gratitude.

'Animals can keep you company, sure, but they aren't people. You need to be around people or you'll end up acting like the animals you spend time with. You need people. A friend, a relative. A woman maybe.'

Adelmo Farandola snorts.

'A relative, then. Forget women, you're right. A relative. That's probably the easiest solution. Do you really not have any living relatives? Maybe a cousin? Even twice or three times removed?'

Adelmo Farandola says nothing, hoping that he will desist. He pretends to stifle a yawn.

'I worry about you,' insists the ranger. 'I'm serious. I worry about you. I don't want you to stay up here alone again this winter.'

'I have everything I need.'

'That's not the point.'

When winter arrives, Adelmo Farandola notices that he seems to have allowed the dog to stay in the cabin, even at night. He watches him curl up at the foot of the bed with a deep sigh. He's become a pet, he thinks. Man's best friend, he thinks. He doesn't know how long it's been going on for. He doesn't know when he stopped giving him the occasional kick just to see him jump, or for the pleasure of being obeyed for no good reason. Go on, punish him, he used to say to himself, even if you don't know what for, he'll know. But now that winter has arrived and the falling snow has begun to erect a white wall around the door and the house, he has lost his taste for disciplining the dog and prefers to keep him by his side. Sometimes he even picks him up, fat and matted as he is, and sits with him on his stomach, like an old rug. The dog, delighted, tries to lick him in gratitude, but Adelmo Farandola turns his face away because he doesn't want to be licked and the dog's saliva leaves a cold trail on his face.

'Ah, my shepherding years...' the dog muses. 'I look back on them fondly. Not the boredom, or the beatings, or the cold, and you do have to take them into account, don't you? I mean, if you're a dog those things are just part of life. No, I miss the work. That nice feeling you got in the evening, the feeling of a job well done. Do you know what I mean? Enjoying it for its own sake. The boss didn't go around handing out compliments, that's for sure – at best, our reward was not getting the usual kick. But that good feeling of a job done perfectly, that little joy – that's what I'm talking about.'

The dog pauses for breath.

'Plus, there was the pleasure of being obeyed. Sheep, cows. I don't know about you, but I've never thought much of that lot. They only know how to obey, and they're not even good at that. You round them up and they scatter. You usher them in one direction and they take fright. You protect them from some danger and they don't even notice. If you leave them alone, they eat, and when they've finished eating everything, they don't even have the sense to move.

They stay there, in the mud, on the stony ground, in their own shit, and they don't understand. Getting them to line up straight was pretty exasperating, although sometimes quite funny. All in all, I got quite fond of them in the end, the stubborn idiots. Of course, they still thought I had it in for them – I let them think so. But what did I care? In the evening, dog-tired, exhausted from running and barking, I knew that I'd done a good job and I went to sleep happy.'

Adelmo Farandola, meanwhile, has nodded off. When he notices, the dog sighs, but doesn't seem disappointed.

At other times, the boredom encourages the dog to share confidences of an altogether different nature.

'Ah, girls! Do you remember them, my friend? I wonder how we get into such a state, restless, sleepless, half-mad, just from the smell of a girl. The delicious stink of some little bitch on the other side of the valley drives us out of our minds. One day we're perfectly calm, concentrating on the important things like food and territory, and the next, quite unexpectedly, we're mad with love, our thingies on fire, our noses going crazy. How can we debase ourselves like that? OK, so it's not the same for you people… for you it's a good thing. But for us – once the mating season comes around and we smell the scent of females on the breeze, nothing else matters. In our frenzy we're happy to be enslaved by that smell again, to howl all night long as we chase after that smell, and be beaten and kicked for howling. Nothing is more important, more beautiful, more desirable. Crawling along, drooling after a female bottom, facing down rivals, overcoming all competition to be her only slave… that's all we crave. Of course, the ones who've been neutered,' the animal rambles on, 'they look down on us, pretending not to understand. They'd rather get fat beside their owners, stretched out at their feet like great rugs. For most of the year we're just the same, but we seem like different species when love descends and shakes us and sets our thingies on fire.'

The dog pauses and drinks from the bowl of drool-flecked water, giving his long tongue a break.

'For the rest of the year, as I say, it's completely different and all we think about is food and faeces like proper gentlemen.'

The snow has completely covered the buildings and silently weighs over everything. Now it really is impossible to leave. The inside of the cabin has slipped into the tense twilight of winter.

'How about a snack?' the dog asks often, in between yawns, his face disappearing behind his tongue.

'You've just eaten.'

'Really? I don't remember.'

'Not long ago. I remember.'

'Ah.' The dog curls up and pretends to concentrate on other things, noisily licking his paws. Then he picks up the conversation again.

'Time for something to eat? What do you say?'

'Shut it.'

Adelmo Farandola has learned to live off very little. He eats only when hunger racks his stomach with long rumbles. The dog, on the other hand, never seems satisfied.

'Yes, well, I suppose that's true,' he agrees when the man points this out.

'You're fat enough already,' the man observes cuttingly.

'I'm not fat. It's just my fur that makes me look bulky.'

'No, you're fat and bloated.'

The dog denies this at length, before giving up.

Rousing himself from one of the waking dreams that populate his days with shadowy figures, Adelmo Farandola catches the dog scratching at the door that connects the cabin and the stable.

'What are you doing?' he shouts.

'Nothing, nothing. I was just passing the time.'

'If I catch you stealing, I'll kick you to death.'

'That's a bit much!'

'I'll do it! You'll see. You're dead!'

They yell at each other for a while, each in his own way, until finally a little snort of laughter escapes, first from one, then from the other.

'Arguing always makes you feel better,' concludes Adelmo Farandola, who is in a philosophical frame of mind.

'I find, for some reason, that arguing gives me an appetite,' says the dog.

Adelmo Farandola has his own thoughts, huge, extensive thoughts as long as whole days, and he finds refuge in day-dreaming. Now, for example, while the dog chatters away, the old man is gathering his memories of hunting in the spring. Ah, spring! There he is, scrambling over the crags, shooting at the chamois, which are still weary from winter.

It's not difficult to hit them: they stand there, stunned, as though expecting to be given a sugar lump. Their arrogant mistrust of the summer is gone and they seem tame, like a flock of grazing animals, only a little timid.

'Look, here I am, here I am,' says Adelmo Farandola as he approaches with a tuft of grass in his hand.

'Look, it's me. How are you?'

The chamois hesitate, confused by the man's friendliness.

Gently, Adelmo Farandola tells them that he's going to kill them, that they won't be able to escape because he'll shoot after them and that'll be even worse, so they might as well get shot in the front.

The animals listen, alert.

'That's how it goes,' he tells them, with as much tenderness as he can muster. 'I hunt and you are hunted.'

He talks to the animals at length, like an ancient warrior talking to his adversary before a duel. When he raises the old shotgun and, unhurried, takes aim, they wait, their thighs twitching nervously. He's promised them a quick and almost pleasant end. He's made them feel that they are part of an inescapable plan. He has demonstrated, through an abundance of arguments, the absurdity of flight and the thousand advantages of surrender.

It's time for the duel.

He fires. His chosen target collapses, while around it others flee in chaos, tripping over rocks and slipping down into the valley as they try to scramble back up. Adelmo Farandola turns to speak to the dying animal. He tells it not to tremble. He tells it to let go, to taste – he uses his own words – the last moments before death. In its death throes, the creature listens to him, its eyes wide with the effort, its tongue sticking out of a corner of its mouth, its nostrils flared, and seems to agree with him.

7

Adelmo Farandola learned the advantages of solitude as a young man, during the time he spent as a fugitive in the woods, among rocky crags and in abandoned mineshafts. He retains vague, distant memories of this period. It was during the war, when the valleys were haunted by men in heavy greatcoats who muttered incomprehensible words as they lined up everyone they came across and shot them without much ceremony. Adelmo Farandola had fled into the mountains like many others who had sensed the danger in time and formed themselves into bands, but he soon went off on his own, wandering among abandoned farms and old mineshafts hidden by tree stumps, eating nothing for days on end except a few berries and leaves that he recognized. He never imagined that he would have to stay hidden for months. He thought it would be only a few days – he thought it would be exciting, like a dangerous children's game.

Day and night he heard the echo of gunfire and he knew that each shot meant the death of another person like him, caught behind a wall, in a mountain pasture or at the bottom of a well. He had heard that the men in greatcoats were methodical and scrupulous, that they knew how to scour the mountainside with binoculars in hand, maps unfurled and the volume on the two-way radio turned all the way up. Sometimes he heard the crackle of those radios, which told him that the grey-coated men were close, really close, so he stopped breathing and tried to still his heartbeat so it couldn't be heard.

Moving from hiding place to hiding place, he eventually came across the abandoned tunnels of a manganese mine, right up beyond the highest pastures, in a harsh, arid little valley full of shattered boulders, where the only living plants were dark shrubs with long, tough roots that even the landslides couldn't dislodge – the valley that, decades later, he would come to own. The old mine's main tunnel was dug into the rock, decorated inside and out with large shells and the fossils of scaly worms, and it became both oesophagus and intestine, swallowing and engulfing him. It was beautiful inside – almost too beautiful. For that reason, he chose a secondary tunnel, barely wider than a rabbit hole, which might have been used in the past to drain water or let in fresh air. He chose it specifically because it was the narrowest. And right there, where the tunnel narrowed so much that you couldn't get through even by crawling, he decided to make his den. The temperature seemed to remain constant in the stony guts of the mine and he comforted himself with the thought that no one, not even the most obstinate grey-coated pursuer, would ever think to look for someone down there, where the rock face oozed putrescence. They would never think to look for him there, in total darkness. Even if they were to venture as far as the valley, they wouldn't spot the mine, since its opening was covered by a tangle of juniper bushes and withered rhododendrons. And even if they did notice the mine, they would only explore the main tunnel and they'd only shine their torches into the mouths of the secondary tunnels, illuminating a few metres at most, and they wouldn't see anyone or anything, and they would give up.

In the war years, Adelmo Farandola learned to find comfort in talking to himself and in imagining the voices of animals and objects ready and willing to reply.

In those years, he learned how to ignore the cold and not feel hunger, how to give both of them the sharp side of his tongue, provoking them into interminable battles of rhetoric and insults.

'You bastards! You bastards!' he would whisper in his tunnel. 'I can't hear you, you bastards. I can't hear you! I'm laughing at you! I can't hear you at all!'

Cold and hunger couldn't talk properly and expressed themselves only with difficulty. At best, they responded with monosyllables and grumblings and gurgles from his exhausted stomach.

'Is that it?' he would say then, curled up at the bottom of his tunnel. 'Is that all you have to say for yourselves? I like feeling hungry. It makes me feel good. It makes me feel light.'

He certainly was light. He felt weightless and transparent, as if his poor skin were made of paper. And like a desert hermit, he took pride in his solitude and raised his voice arrogantly, hearing the bowels of the mine reverberate, not realizing that his voice was barely a hoarse whisper, without an echo, and his words were little more than white breaths in the freezing darkness.

His rhetoric was simple, drawn from his memories of similar verbal battles with young men from other villages, when they used to provoke each other in front of the girls. Adelmo Farandola and those young men used to come to blows quickly, because words were one thing but fists another, and fists were generally more effective, whirling left, right and centre.

He would call these young men impotent, queer, sons of peasants and sons of bitches: burning insults that got his rivals fired up and goaded them into fighting. It seemed to work the same with cold and hunger. Adelmo Farandola insulted Hunger's mother, Cold's mother and Sleep's mother too. Sleep, the most treacherous enemy, seemed like a friend but really wanted nothing more than for Adelmo Farandola to let himself go, in order to hand him over to Death. Adelmo added a touch of blasphemy to his insults and he heard them rising to the heavens, powerful beams of dark light flying upwards as though through a chimney. In reality, they were barely sighs: his voice caught in his throat as he spoke in a gasp that broke before he reached the final syllable.

He slapped Cold and Hunger around, boasting that they weren't making him suffer enough, and invited them to do better, because he didn't mind having a bit of an appetite, and in fact he was feeling a trifle warm. He was ashamed – yes, ashamed – to have such hesitant enemies, such pale and mediocre adversaries.

'Is that all you're going to do?' he wheezed. 'Is that all you can do to me?'

He laughed as hard as he could, a vulgar laugh, putting himself in danger of being heard by his real enemies, the ones outside, who were hunting him through all the valley's nooks and crannies, tracking down the fugitives and rebels one by one in order to execute them on the spot. His enemies couldn't have heard him, of course, since his voice was a faltering breath, a death rattle, but Adelmo didn't know that, and in his heart he believed he was defying them as well.

Hunger, Cold and Sleep sat in front of him, wrapped in dark rags. They had normal faces and tired expressions. They had run out of arguments and looked sidelong at one another with evident unease.

'Would you like to go?' Adelmo Farandola said, laughing in his fever. 'No, stay and keep me company! Don't go or I'll be offended! That's the sort of man I am.'

And so, triumphing over the squalid eloquence of Hunger and Cold and Sleep, Adelmo Farandola survived and escaped the clutches of the soldiers in the heavy grey coats.

People imagine that a snow-covered mountain must be a silent realm. But snow and ice are noisy, mocking, unabashed creatures. Everything creaks under the weight of the snow, and the creaking takes your breath away, because it seems like the prelude to a devastating collapse. The sound of snow and ice settling echoes for a long time, travelling through the ground underfoot and through the air. The great avalanches speak in fearsome roars that fill the listener with dread and in fierce hisses of displaced air – but even the smaller landslides thunder and echo through the valleys, the sound vibrating between rock walls miles away from the actual point of collapse.

Footsteps squeak painfully on fresh snow and each step seems like a sob. Each individual snowflake strikes the windows and surfaces with a nervous little noise, like the sound of a page turning in an overly long book. And when the temperature grows less frigid, the huge blocks of ice shriek until they shatter, are overtaken by fits of coughing and indulge in thunderous, flatulent outbursts.

To Adelmo Farandola, buried under the snow, these are the familiar sounds of the eternal winter. In the cabin, buried under the weight of metres of snow, they sound muffled but audible, and the din that carries on night and day seems to modulate like music scored for several voices.

Some are hostile – decidedly malicious. Others are more ingratiating, even – sometimes – touched by a kind of tenderness. Adelmo Farandola never replies to the first kind, since replying only makes it worse: they come closer and get more arrogant, and threaten terrible things, although they don't go into specifics. He doesn't mind answering the second sort. He knows that they won't go too far – at worst they'll make fun of him and he won't realize until later, when he turns it over and over in his mind.

'If you say so,' Adelmo Farandola says offhandedly to an icy borborygmus.

Or 'Yes, of course,' to a distant crash – too far away to be really menacing.

The drip-drip-dripping which, in the daytime, seems to herald the arrival of spring makes him laugh and exasperates him a bit. 'Well, are we going to put an end to it or not?' he asks, in an exaggerated parody of irritation.

'I beg your pardon?' says the dog, misunderstanding.

'I wasn't talking to you,' says Adelmo Farandola.

'You weren't?'

'No. Go on, shoo!'

Every so often, Adelmo Farandola remembers about the cables that buzzed above his head all through his childhood. The houses in the village where he was born were huddled together right under the path of the power line between two pylons and, high over their heads, the cables buzzed night and day. When the wind dropped and sleep quietened the ringing of the cowbells, the buzzing increased until it absorbed all thought. When that happened, men worried that they were going mad and screamed so as not to hear the buzzing in their heads; they beat their women and beat their animals; they drank bottle after bottle of wine, hoping they would go deaf; they went out into the fields and never returned. 'We're all going mad,' his poor mother had said. And his father said so too, before picking up a large stick and chasing after his son as though the buzzing was his fault. 'All mad, all mad,' said the inhabitants of the village, who held the cables responsible for every evil that befell them, forgetting about the endless blows they'd suffered before the workmen had come from outside the village to construct the pylons and hang the cables. Animals died for no good reason, or went mad in the fields and gored one another with their horns, and their young (not all of them, it's true, only some of them) were stillborn or deformed. 'It's the cables, the cables,' his mother said, crossing herself.

Adelmo Farandola has been convinced for some time that if there's something not quite right in his head it's to do with the years he spent living under the cables of the power line. I've gone mad, I've gone mad, he repeats to himself expressionlessly, as though it were a normal observation, because those cables had to happen to someone after all, and they happened to him.

'Am I mad?' he asks the dog.

'Well, I'd say you're a bit odd, yes.'

'It's those high-voltage cables.'

The dog looks up and doesn't see any.

'What cables?'

'The ones from when I was a boy.'

8

There's someone who knocks at the door during the long winter days. Adelmo Farandola hears the knocking at night – or perhaps during the day, because night and day tend to blend together beneath the layers of snow that transform light into a pale blue gloom. Adelmo Farandola jumps.

'Who's there?' he asks, and then pretends not to be at home because he doesn't like having strangers around, and stays perfectly still.

More knocks at the door.

'Who's there?' asks the old man, his voice little more than a whisper, because he doesn't really want to know who's knocking. He stays still and silent, breathing hesitantly.

The dog watches him, waiting.

'What should I do? Should I bark?' he asks.

'No, don't move.'

'My instinct is to bark.'

'I know, but don't. They'll go away soon.'

'You think?'

The dog awaits the next knocks anxiously, his ears pricked up. There they are. He lets slip a snarl.

'No!' Adelmo Farandola orders. 'Or I'll kick you to death.'

The dog whines in frustration.

At night, the knocking is slower and fainter. It's the snow knocking, the thick layer of snow that has enveloped the entire cabin, hiding it from the sun, reducing it to a little bump on the smooth surface. It's the snow asking to come in.

Adelmo Farandola is woken by the knocking. He sleeps lightly – since his days as a fugitive during the war, it doesn't take much to wake him up, and afterwards he spends hours staring fixedly into the darkness, waiting to fall back to sleep. But these knocks are so faint and distant that he doesn't know if he's really heard them or if he dreamed them, and he doesn't even know if he's really awake now or if he's dreaming of being awake. In these moments, in the damp darkness of the cold cabin, he feels as though he's back in the cave from his youth, down at the bottom of the tunnel in the manganese mine. And he's afraid to move and let a hand or an elbow touch the rock walls that constrict and engulf him and swallow him up like a great stomach.

'You hear them too?' he asks the dog during the day. It's a relief to confirm that he's not dreaming them.

'Of course I hear them too,' says the dog.

'That's good.'

'What should I do, then? Should I bark?'

'No, no.'

The snow weighing down on them moves and lives and breathes. The knocking shows that it's alive. Now that it's enveloped them, it's taking its time to digest them. That's what the old man sometimes thinks. He prefers not to tell the dog about this feeling, because he can see he's anxious and scared enough as it is, ready to panic at the least creak or drip. How will he react to the ice crashing down in spring, the man wonders, since he's already so frightened by the least little thing?

Sometimes the knocking comes from the stable.

'The cows,' Adelmo Farandola says, sitting up.

'Cows?' The dog yawns.

Adelmo Farandola has suddenly remembered about the milking schedule. He jumps up from the bed, wraps an extra blanket around his shoulders and opens the stable door.

'Cows, eh?' says the dog.

'They've all escaped,' the old man whispers.

'The whole time I've known you I've never seen cows in there.'

Adelmo Farandola looks around him, bewildered. There are only provisions: crates of apples and potatoes, sacks of flour, bottles, logs, useless tools.

'My cows,' he murmurs again.

The dog has already gone back into the cabin, where there's still a bit of warmth.

And yet there is something that moves in the dark stable, as soon as the door to the cabin is closed. There's a rummaging, a slithering, the squeaking of chains and rings. Cracks, little thumps, screeches. Adelmo Farandola listens to it for a long time, but resists the temptation to get up again to go and see. The dog hears it too, with trembling, nervous ears, but he pretends to be asleep and doesn't move.

'It's the cables, the cables of the power line,' Adelmo Farandola murmurs, faced with the voices and the shadows.

He thinks he hears the cables buzzing with current, the noise that used to follow him everywhere, even when in reality it was just the hum of grasshoppers in the fields or the drone of engines rising up from the roads at the bottom of the valley.

'Those cables are driving me mad,' he says to himself, and glances out of the window, as though he could see them, and just at that moment he thinks he really does see them beyond the wall of snow: long trails of live, chattering cables.

'The money, the money,' Adelmo Farandola mutters occasionally in his sleep. In his dreams, he is forced to chase after banknotes fluttering in the breeze, or to hunt for a stash hidden God knows where and forgotten. He keeps muttering 'the money, the money' even after he's woken up, in the dark of the cabin.

Since the sale of the first valley, Adelmo Farandola has always kept an old suitcase of banknotes near at hand by his side. There is more money in a bank account, as per the wishes of his brother, who is sharper and more shrewd, but Adelmo Farandola has forgotten about that – it's too far away, too abstract. The damp notes in the suitcase buried in the stable are what he uses to buy his provisions.

'The money, the money,' Adelmo Farandola mutters as he pulls first one, then two blankets over his shoulders and opens the stable door. He remembers that the money is safely in there. But each time he is compelled to spend hours looking for it, throwing the crates of potatoes and apples around, rummaging in the woodpile, excavating the manure-soaked soil. The dog watches him from the door and yawns.

When he finds it at last, he stays there staring at it for a long time, not knowing what to do. His relief at finding it is quickly replaced by a sense of weariness. Adelmo Farandola knows that he must hide it again, as soon as possible, to stop anyone from finding it while he's away. He walks round and round the stable with the suitcase in his hand, searching for a hiding place that he would never think to check and that he will forget almost immediately.

During that long winter under the snow, so long that it almost becomes a kind of eternity, during the frozen days which turn into nights without him realizing it, Adelmo Farandola lets sleep and waking blend together. The characters who come to meddle in his dreams end up staying with him during the day as well. Sometimes, the cabin seems to be visited by a whole raft of people. They come and go, wandering around, full of curiosity. They're people from the village, for the most part, dressed in autumn or spring clothes – the times of year when he goes down to the village to get provisions. They greet him with a wave or a smile as they pass in front of him, but he doesn't deign to reply. Sometimes they chat to other characters who belong to other times. These are people Adelmo Farandola knew years ago and who come back to visit him in silence. Relatives, including distant ones and ones who aren't really family, childhood friends and a couple of timid young women who might – he's not sure, he doesn't remember – have been particular friends of his and who might – only might – have made his heart beat faster.

He also spots a few unknown figures, tall and silent, who hang around him as if waiting for him to speak. Adelmo Farandola stubbornly resists and doesn't say a word until at last they step back and fade away.

In certain pools further down the valley, in high summer, the red mountain frogs deposit clouds of frogspawn. The sun warms the water little by little, nurturing the mucilaginous eggs. Finally, around July, thousands of tadpoles appear more or less simultaneously and start to wriggle in the muddy water. There are too many for the little pools. Soon they crowd onto the banks, propelling themselves with squishy force. Then they begin to bite one another, forming groups and attacking one at a time, ripping each other to shreds in a thrashing of tails and a gnashing of toothless mouths.

Adelmo Farandola imagines going down to where the pools are slowly drying up in the sun and the arid air, to watch the tadpoles. He describes them to the dog, who listens with great curiosity.

'Well I never,' says the dog. 'What sort of thing are they?'

'Frogs.'

'I'd never have guessed.'

'Newborn frogs. And you should see them eating each other. Unbelievable. Why do they do that?'

'How should I know?'

'Probably they don't have enough space. It's a horrible sight, I'm telling you.'

'Why don't you stop them?' the dog ventures.

Adelmo Farandola sniggers and bends down to see the floor better, as if the pool teeming with tadpoles were in front of him right there and then in the cabin. Next to him, the dog sniffs the air, trying to pick up their scent.

'What do they smell like?' he asks at last.

'Let's see, hmm... a smell like... well, it's a sort of... hmm... how can I describe it?'

'Never mind.'

Adelmo Farandola puts out a hand, dips it into the imaginary water like a scoop and draws it back full of writhing tadpoles.

'Are they happy?' asks the dog, who can almost see them. 'They seem to be wagging their tails.'

'Happy? I wouldn't know. Want some?'

'Sorry?' asks the dog.

'A little taste?'

'Are you joking? What do you take me for?'

Adelmo Farandola laughs and mimes shoving the tadpoles in his mouth.

'Now, what would you say if I did that?' the dog asks reprovingly.

'Your loss. They're not bad.'

Adelmo Farandola swallows them without chewing, alive and raw. A smile crosses his face as he feels them wriggling down his throat.

'There they are,' he says after a while, meaning that they've arrived in his stomach.

Another handful, another mouthful. The dog watches him, unsure whether to drool or not.

'I might,' says the dog after the third handful, 'almost be tempted to try some myself.'

'Please, go ahead,' says Adelmo Farandola. 'After what I've just had I don't need dinner.'

The dog lowers his muzzle and roots around in the non-existent mucilage waving at the edge of the pool. He lifts his head, chewing slowly.

'Well?' asks the old man.

'Bah,' says the dog.

'You have to get used to these things. We'll try again tomorrow. You'll find that they'll be a bit better than today. That's how it was for me too. You have to give it time.'

'If you say so.'

The dog gives his nose a lick to get rid of the putrid smell that the idea of stagnant water has left behind. He looks at Adelmo Farandola and seems to feel compassion for him.

9

'Melt, melt,' Adelmo Farandola implores, standing by the window, because as of yesterday there's no more food.

'Melt, melt,' the dog whines, remembering Adelmo Farandola's old intention of eating him.

With two mouths to feed instead of one, the food supplies have run out early. In spite of rationing, the bread, cheese and sausages ran out days ago. The potatoes, apples, dried meat, rotten meat, bones and skin are gone too.

'What do we do now?' asks the dog anxiously.

'We wait,' says Adelmo Farandola, who can see nothing beyond the glass but the usual wall of gloomy azure snow.

The dog decides not to mention the lack of food for now. He doesn't want to encourage the old man's imagination.

'Are you hungry?' the man asks, trying to make conversation.

'No, no, not at all!' the dog says with a yawn, as though this were was just idle chat. But they are both kept awake at night by the groans coming from their empty stomachs, which move and contract as if they wanted to come up out of their mouths to go looking for food themselves.

Two days without eating, then three. There's no shortage of water, all they have to do is open the door and collect some snow in a saucepan and melt it over the stove. But soon Adelmo Farandola is hunting for crumbs with his nose on the ground.

'Um, have you lost something?' asks the dog.

'Crumbs.'

'Oh, right. I'm afraid I've already mopped them up,' says the dog. 'If I'd known I would have left you some.'

They search the corners of the cabin and then the stable, several times. Every tiny fragment of food is intercepted and eaten. Adelmo Farandola licks the inside of the polenta pan, which still holds a trace of the accumulated grease of many years, an aroma – or at least the nostalgia for an aroma.

They are forced to go to bed earlier than before, because in their sleep they can escape their gnawing hunger; but even in their dreams they are haunted by an inhuman craving, eternally delayed meals and the tortures of Tantalus.

Adelmo Farandola gets up several times a day, crosses from the bed to the window, checks the level of the snow and goes back to bed without saying a word. Even the dog has lost the will to speak. He stays curled up and heaves sighs of protest.

'Stop that!' the old man bursts out at last.

'What was I doing?'

'Complaining.'

'No, I wasn't. Although I'd have every reason to. First you invite me to stay, then you find out you don't have enough food for two. You're an idiot.'

'If I catch you, I'm cooking you.'

The dog snorts and doesn't move. He knows that by now the man is too weak.

A few more days pass. Exhausted, the man and the dog stare at each other from their respective corners. Whoever survives will eat the other one and will have enough to keep going until the thaw. But the thought of ending up as food keeps them both alive. I won't give you the satisfaction, they both think. I'm stronger than you.

With infinite slowness, Adelmo Farandola puts a resinous log on the fire. Then he gets to work boiling up the ancient slabs of manure that cover the stable floor. Then, methodically, he starts eating the flakes of grime that have developed on his body through years of perspiration. They taste unimaginably awful, but they seem nourishing. He picks at himself with his nails, revealing traces of incredibly white skin underneath.

The dog watches his every move with rapt attention.

'Can I have a little lick?' he pleads.

'No,' says Adelmo Farandola. But finally, overcome by a nausea that prevents him from carrying on, he allows the dog to taste him.

Day, night, day, night.

It's still snowing, all through the night sometimes. Then, during the day, a warm, violent wind compresses the fallen snow, alternating with the icy night air which freezes it, leaving it rock-hard. Whenever a certain mildness in the air seems to announce that the worst will soon be over, new clouds start massing, fresh snow falls on top of the frozen layer, new avalanches come crashing haphazardly down from the peaks, falling where they like, flattening forests and sawing the tops off trees. But at last, even this endless, dragging winter draws to a close. Inside the cabin, an exhausted Adelmo Farandola senses that their captivity beneath the snow is about to end. He hears it in the crash of the ice as it splinters, in the wail of the frozen crust as it scrapes and grinds, in the drip-drip-dripping that starts before first light and doesn't stop until dusk.

'We're getting there, we're getting there,' he says to himself, feeding the fire with the last scraps of wood and paper. 'We're getting there,' he sings under his breath to the dog, who listens to him drowsily, unable to move.

Day by day, the level of the snow falls. One morning, as he opens the window, Adelmo Farandola realizes that a blindingly bright ray of light is shining into the room from above the frozen ice. The twilight gloom he and the dog have inhabited for five months is suddenly gone, destroyed by a single sunbeam glimmering with dust motes. Alarmed, the dog barks at the intruder, gazing in terror at the fiery dust. Adelmo Farandola doesn't know whether to laugh at this reaction or scoff, like he scoffs at the annoying people who try to come into his house, looking for old benches or Alpine cheeses.

'Winter's over,' says Adelmo Farandola.

'Oh, right,' says the dog. 'I must have misunderstood.'

'We'll be able to go out soon. Are you pleased?'

The dog sticks out his tongue and bows his head. He doesn't know what to say. The sun has returned to shed its light on the valley but the snow is still metres high and it will still take time, days and days. But, they both think, it will be satisfying to piss and shit outside again, on the grass and the soil, and feel the breeze tickling their dicks after five months spent pissing and shitting indoors in a bucket and emptying it into a horizontal hole dug in the snow immediately outside the door. The dog thinks how nice and satisfying it will be to go back to his favourite spots and mark them with the smell of his own piss, since you never know when someone's going to challenge your territory. Then again, neither of them has anything left to piss or shit after going so long without eating.

Day by day, the snow beyond the window retreats and so does the snow by the door. At last you can see the outside world – a world made of dazzling white and light blue and grey, with no other features. An incessant dripping comes from the roof, keeping them awake and unable to concentrate. Long, lamenting, drawn-out roars come from the mountains around them, and crashing noises, each one louder than the last. Finally the day comes for the two of them to take a couple of steps outside the cabin, in the already muddy snow. With each step, the old man sinks up to his thighs. The dog, lighter, walks on the hardened crust, but sometimes he treads on a more unstable patch by accident and plunges in up to his ears and thrashes around, panicking, which makes the man laugh.

'Stop that,' the man tells him.

'Help! I'm dying!' the dog shrieks.

'What do I care?'

'Don't leave me! I'm dying!'

In the end the dog emerges from the abyss, spitting snow, and shakes himself before falling in again, moaning again, and laughing in spite of himself.

'I'm going back inside,' he says at last. But he doesn't move.

The pure, cold air has left them dazed. They stand there, drunk on air and light, and they almost forget about food.

'Is it always like this?' asks the dog.

'Who can remember a thing like that? I think so. It's worth it, isn't it?'

Adelmo Farandola means: it's worth rotting away inside for an entire season, it's worth risking death from starvation, just to feel this, to get drunk on whiteness and cleanliness. The dog nods, happy and confused.

In their ancient wisdom, the previous inhabitants of the valley were careful to build the cabin on a strip of land where avalanches never fall. Adelmo Farandola has been able to test this over the years. The avalanches come down on either side of the cabin, they spill over and get very close, hurling heaps of earth and ice and rock almost as far as the threshold, but they don't go further than that.

The old man observes the greyish, shapeless mass of snow and earth with satisfaction. There are bits of detritus sticking out from it, branches, tree trunks, poles and enormous rocks. The dog starts sniffing around, heading towards the remains of an avalanche that came down to the right of the cabin one day last month. They both remember that day, and the terrible noise that left them breathless. They remember the shaking which almost knocked them to the ground and rattled the stone walls as though they were sheets of tin, and knocked two bottles off a shelf. They both remember the churning, roaring gust that passed over the roof and spared them only because the house was already protected by a thick, solid layer of old snow.

'What are you sniffing for?' asks the man.

'I can smell something,' says the dog.

'You're always smelling something.'

'Yes, but this is strong. See if you can smell it.'

'I can't smell anything.'

'Use your eyes, then.'

They approach the foot of the avalanche. Adelmo Farandola is pleased because he has already guessed what might have caught the dog's attention. Over time, bodies of dead animals always emerge from the heaps of fallen snow: fleeing chamois, ibexes and goats, torn to pieces by the avalanche but kept fresh by the ice. He takes advantage of nature's generosity and extracts the carcasses from the snow, piece by piece, and cooks them up, because by spring the sausages have long since run out, the tinned meat is no more than a distant memory, and the legs and ribs and necks of those chamois and ibexes are well preserved. Once they've been de-haired and had the soil scrubbed off they're good; even the bones make a good broth, which he colours with a glass of wine – if there's any wine left.

'What animal is that?' he asks the dog.

The dog doesn't speak.

'Can't you tell what animal it is?'

'That's not an animal,' the dog whispers, motionless.

10

It's a human foot, not a hoof, that the man and the dog can see sticking out of the debris from the avalanche. It sticks up like a seedling that's made its way doggedly and laboriously through layer after layer of soil, before unfurling and growing stronger in the fresh air and the sunlight. It's grey with soil and badly bruised.

'It's a foot,' says Adelmo Farandola.

'It's one of your lot,' says the dog.

'Well I never. Who knows how long it's been under there?'

'The avalanche spares no one,' says the dog, like someone who knows what he's talking about.

'What do you know about it?'

'That's what they say. Should I investigate?'

The dog is ready to leap into action, to plunge his paws into the snow and dig until they bleed.

'You'd never manage it, idiot,' the old man says. 'You'd only hurt yourself.'

'That doesn't matter. I'm happy to do it.'

'You're not a St Bernard.'

'No, thank God. Have you seen how they drool?'

They stand there, staring at the blackened foot, until they both think they see it move.

'It moved!'

'No, it didn't. You're imagining it.'

'Maybe he's still alive down there.'

'Shut it.'

'You don't think so?'

'He's dead. The avalanche spares no one.'

'Exactly, that's just what I said!'

'For all I know, if there's one foot here, the other might be ten metres away over there, and as for the arms –'

'I get it. I get it.'

'We'd better wait.'

'Wait for what?' asks the dog.

'For the snow to melt. For the foot to come free. In a month we'll know more.'

'And we'll collect the pieces. In the meantime, what should we do? Do you want to say a few words?'

'Like what?'

'A prayer. Isn't that what you people do?'

'I don't know any prayers.'

'You don't say.'

'I mean, I don't remember a single one.'

'Don't you have a what-do-you-call-it in your house? A prayer book?'

'Never had one.'

The dog walks in a circle, indecisive. Then, in deference to the situation, he goes to piss on the trunk of a half-buried tree.

The smell of earth and rot that accompanies the thaw becomes so strong that it keeps them both awake at night, the dog and the man. The snow retreats, revealing the bodies of animals crushed by the avalanche or taken unawares by cold and hunger. It leaves them to warm up in the faint spring sunshine, letting the flavoursome gases that rise in coils from the cadavers summon the first swarms of insects.

They arrive buzzing, and settle down to lick and suck at the carcasses' reeking limbs. They are followed by the birds, ready to devour anything to relieve their hunger, and the first carnivores, foxes and weasels, woken in their dens by the scent. They scurry up to the carcasses and sniff them at length, enraptured, before allowing themselves a bite. They encourage the youngest ones to have a taste and allow older ones who have survived the winter to choose their own morsels.

Sometimes, while hunting among the ice for freshly emerged food, an animal will suddenly come across the remains of one of its own kind. When this happens, it sniffs at the body in a different way, as though recognizing a friend or a relative, and nudges it with its muzzle, seemingly trying to wake it from an overlong hibernation. It won't take a bite unless hunger has left it confused and indifferent to the simple but enduring taboos of nature. Sometimes these little gestures of nose and muzzle seem like a conversation between old friends who haven't seen each other for a while.

'I love this stink,' says the dog when they emerge into the fresh air to fetch provisions and are almost blinded by the light.

'What stink?'

'This one. Decomposition. Earth, mud, excrement. And then the first flowers. Perhaps I'm sentimental, but I find this stink moving.'

He bounds away happily over the patches of snow, his tongue hanging out, and charges into the clumps of pallid, newly emerged grass, before running off to frighten the other animals who have flocked to the banquet.

Standing immobile on the threshold of his cabin, Adelmo Farandola watches him and thinks that he would do the same if he were twenty years younger.

The next day, as they are stocking up on meat from the animals torn apart by avalanches, Adelmo Farandola stumbles across a foot sticking out of the front of a snowdrift.

'Look,' he says to the dog in bemusement.

'It's the foot from yesterday,' says the dog.

'Seriously?'

'Don't you remember?'

'No. Well, sort of, but I thought I'd dreamed it.'

'It's the foot from yesterday, I'm telling you.'

'And what should we do? What did we decide to do yesterday?'

'Nothing. Wait for the thaw.'

'Really?'

'Yes. To be honest, I didn't really agree, but you…'

After a few days the old man discovers the foot again.

'A foot!'

'Will you stop that! It's still the same foot as before!' shouts the dog, exasperated.

'Oh, that wasn't a dream?'

'Give me strength,' says the dog.

'What should we do? What did we say we'd do before?'

This time the dog tries to take advantage of the situation.

'We decided that we should dig down and free the rest of the body.'

'Really?'

'I could have sworn we did,' says the dog.

'It seems strange that we should decide to do something like that.'

'Well, there it is.'

'Very strange. We'll never manage it.'

'We'll wait for the thaw instead,' says Adelmo Farandola, when the dog brings it up again. 'We can't do anything for that man. He's dead, he's in pieces. Besides, the snow is too hard because it's mixed in with ice and rock, and climbing over the snow to get to the foot is too dangerous because you could get submerged. And if you start digging with your paws, you'll just get something lodged in there and ruin your feet. Besides, we're weak. It's been a long winter and we're not in good shape. Let's wait.'

So they wait, day after day. But every morning, when a sliver of sunlight filters in through the grimy windowpane and gives them the signal, they leave the cabin and go to see how the thaw is coming along.

The foot is still there, blackened and dry like a lightning-struck sapling. It's no longer a novelty for the old man, but every time he sees it it's like a long-distant memory come to life.

'How long do you think it's been there?' he asks one morning.

'You're asking me?'

'How many years has it been there?'

'Years? What's wrong with you? It can't be more than a week,' says the dog, who, in truth, doesn't know how to count the days.

'We should do something,' the dog says again. 'That thing's starting to stink too much.'

'I can't smell anything.'

'I can. And if I can smell it, so can the others.'

'Which others?'

'Other dogs. My colleagues. Animals. Birds. Those bastard feral cats. Wolves. Don't you remember what your ranger friend was saying? Are there really wolves round here?'

'Dunno. What friend?'

'What do you mean you don't know? Have you never seen one? It's not hard: either you've seen one or you haven't. For example, I saw one once. Not here, don't worry, in another valley a long way away. But if I saw one there, I might see one here too. Those guys like to move around. And if I saw one, we could see ten of them. Those guys run in packs.'

Adelmo Farandola gets bored quickly and the dog chatters too much.

'Shut up. There's no wolves here. I'll tell you what we'll do. We'll keep an eye on the foot during the day. It's not as though we have much else to do.'

'During the day? And at night? Listen, friend, we're talking about animals here. Those guys prefer to go looking for food at night. Do you understand what I'm saying?'

'I sleep at night. Are you going to spend your nights outside keeping watch over the foot?'

'No, wait, that's not what I meant.'

'Do you want to stay out at night?' Adelmo Farandola goads him, using his stern voice.

'No, no, that's the last thing I want,' the dog whimpers.

Bit by bit, the thaw allows more avalanche debris to emerge: more paws, more horns, more tree trunks, muzzles that are all teeth, skulls still wearing the disoriented expressions of their final moments.

'It's like watching a beard grow,' Adelmo Farandola says one day.

'In what sense?'

'Hairs. These bits of things, these paws. They sprout like hairs.'

'Oh, I see,' says the dog, who doesn't see.

'Human hairs, I mean,' says the old man.

'Of course, of course.' Then: 'Should we go down and let someone know?'

'Who?'

'I don't know. People like you. People in the village.'

Adelmo Farandola stares ahead of him, where the floor of his valley plunges down in rills and scree slopes towards the bottom of the main valley.

'Too much snow,' he says. 'Better wait.'

'Right, then. Let's wait. But that foot there makes me a little anxious,' says the dog.

'Still too much snow, I'm telling you. Do you want to kill yourself on the way down?'

Some days later they re-examine the question.

'With a pair of snowshoes you could easily go down along the path we followed to get up here and –'

'What's the hurry, dog? You see him? He's dead. He can wait. And so can we.'

11

The cold, white sun is blinding, but it doesn't seem able to melt the snow. On the contrary, it seems to caress it gently, remoulding it where it looks as though it might cave in, reinforcing it and making it more compact.

The days pass. To appease the dog, the old man goes to see if a path to the lower valley has opened up. But further down, the icy snow glimmers like a layer of marble between the trees.

'Do you know what I was thinking?' says the dog. 'We could tell that ranger who used to come and see you in the autumn.'

Adelmo Farandola struggles to put his memories and ideas back in order before replying.

'He wasn't coming to see me. He was spying on me.'

'Whatever. Him. Perhaps... perhaps he'll be able to get up here before we can move. That's his job, isn't it? Perhaps... perhaps he'll come up here with one of those flying things that you people use in the mountains... What do you call them?'

'Helicopters.'

'Yeah, those things. He can land here, in the meadow, and there you go. You tell him what's what, that you've found this foot, and that you really wanted to tell someone about it straight away but…'

Adelmo Farandola shakes his head.

'He would think for sure that I'd done it,' he murmurs.

'What an idea! Of course you didn't do it! You? Kill the man on the end of that foot? On purpose? Come on, how could he think that? How could he?'

The old man keeps silent because he doesn't remember anything.

'It wasn't you, was it?' the dog asks.

'No, no,' Adelmo Farandola snaps.

Brief showers of snow seem to turn back time, muddling up the seasons. They draw a veil over the foot, hiding it from view for a day or two. When that happens, Adelmo Farandola manages to forget about the foot and the man attached to it, and wanders freely around the meadow, careful not to sink beneath the snow.

The dog follows him silently, sometimes running ahead, only to come back with the fur on his stomach bristling with little clumps of snow.

But the effects of these snow showers don't last long. Soon the foot is freed again, more blackened and twisted than ever, and the thought of the foot and of the man hidden under the debris returns to hammer on Adelmo Farandola's temples.

'We really should tell someone about it,' he says.

'Exactly, exactly, exactly!' barks the dog. 'Shall we do it now?'

'Tomorrow.'

'But you said "tomorrow" the day before yesterday!'

'Really?'

When the path down to the valley begins to clear, turning back into stone and mud, Adelmo Farandola decides that the moment has come to head down. He slips several times, falling on his arse and giving himself bruises that will last for weeks, and he swears every time he puts a foot wrong and sinks up to the knee in a pool of freezing mud and snow. The dog, by his side, seems to see the whole thing in a different light. Blissfully, he covers himself in dirt, drinks mud, rolls in the blackened snow, laughing, and puts his nose to the ground, chasing after the stench of the first animals to have ventured outside their dens.

Halfway there, however, when they've almost reached the bottom of the copse of larches, they find that a landslide of snow and earth has cut across the path, at a point that was steep enough to begin with, making it impossible to continue. Adelmo Farandola tries another way: it descends for a few metres between some larches clinging to a rock face which, seen from above, appears almost vertical. He's soon forced to climb back up, however, spluttering with the effort, because he's in serious danger of killing himself.

'Watch out!' barks the dog, who's stayed behind to keep guard over the last stretch of the path.

'It's impossible from here,' the old man concludes, sitting in the mud to get his breath back.

'Are you all right?'

'It was a close-run thing, I tell you.'

The dog sighs.

'We'll try again in a couple of days,' he says. 'Let's go back up. We can take a look at that foot. Have you ever seen such a thing…'

A few days of spring warmth melt more chunks of snow and open up new routes. Adelmo Farandola gets ready before dawn and makes his way down the path, eventually reaching the first vegetable patches outside the village.

The houses, sunk in the deep shadow that hangs over the lower valley until late March, seem deserted. I wonder what day it is, the man thinks.

'What day is it?' he asks the dog.

'How should I know? It's today.'

Adelmo Farandola heads to the shop where he usually gets his provisions, followed by the dog, who is determined to sniff every nook and cranny of the village. It's closed.

The old man calls out. There's no answer. He calls again and rattles the door. Still nothing. The dog helps him by barking, but the village is full of dogs who bark at the slightest hint of movement and people have stopped paying attention to barking dogs.

After a while, the lady appears in a window right above the shop.

'What's the matter? Oh, it's you,' she says, surprised and sleepy.

'Good morning,' says Adelmo Farandola, suddenly shy. 'Do you know what time it is?'

'No.'

'Do you know what day it is?'

'No. I…'

The lady retreats and the window is closed once more. Disheartened, Adelmo Farandola is about to turn back when she reappears, speaking to him through the door of the shop, which she has opened a crack.

'You mustn't surprise me like that,' she says. 'Come in. But leave the dog outside.'

Adelmo Farandola thanks her and glances at the dog, who understands at once and sits; then he takes off his hat and steps into the dark shop with his head bowed. He keeps his eyes fixed on the ground because the lady is wearing a dressing gown and underneath she might be naked. Perhaps it's Sunday, he thinks. Early on Sunday morning. I should have worked it out before coming down, he thinks.

'Well?' says the lady, without smiling. She's left the door open.

'Well?'

'Your provisions ran out sooner than you were expecting this winter. What exactly do you need?'

'Ah, well. To tell the truth, nothing.'

The lady is silent.

'Well, that is – I need all sorts of things but,' Adelmo Farandola continues, 'I came down because… I saw…'

He struggles to find words when he feels overwhelmed. They slip out of his mind and he ends up with a clear idea in his head and no words to express it.

'What did you see?'

'A foot.'

One of the lady's cheeks twitches in surprise.

'A foot,' she repeats.

'Yes, a foot. A man's foot.'

'I see.'

'A foot in the snow.'

'A footprint, you mean?'

'No, no, a foot sticking out of the snow.'

The lady listens, her hands folded, her gaze fixed, her mouth tight, repressing a yawn.

'An accident,' she says at last.

'Yes, that's it. I think. An accident.'

'But do you mean someone's been hurt, or...'

'Dead. I mean that someone's dead.'

'Are you sure?'

'Yes. I've never seen it move.'

Adelmo Farandola prefers not to mention that he's actually seen the foot wave several times and heard the hooked toes creak.

'Hmm,' says the lady. 'And why did you come to tell me?'

'Because... I don't know,' says Adelmo Farandola. 'I don't know many people here in the village.'

'But listen, why didn't you go to the police station and drag one of the carabinieri out of bed? Although, on a Sunday there's no guarantee...'

Adelmo Farandola passes a hand across his eyes.

'Yes, go to them. The more I think about it, the more I'm sure it's the only thing to do. That way, if you need to report a disappearance...'

'I'm not reporting a disappearance. I'm talking about a discovery.'

'It's the same thing, isn't it? People come, people go. Perhaps they – the carabinieri, I mean – have a list of missing people... But are you certain of what you saw?'

Adelmo Farandola clears his throat, hesitating. He's starting to forget why he's there.

'Well?' the lady presses him.

'Well what?'

'What exactly did you see?'

'Where?'

'In the snow! The foot!'

'The foot? You've seen it too?'

'No, you did! Come on! Pull yourself together!'

Without knowing why, he lets a half-smile escape him, which the lady immediately interprets as evidence of a joke.

'Oh, very good,' she says. 'Very good! Aren't we funny. Let's play the fool. Shall *I* call the carabinieri, then?'

'Why didn't you help me out earlier, when I was struggling?' Adelmo Farandola asks the dog as they plod back up the slippery path towards the cabin. 'We'd have explained it better between the two of us.'

'Well, I'm sorry, but I was stuck outside. I couldn't even hear what you were saying.'

'Rubbish. You could have helped me explain. I just made myself look like an idiot in there.'

'And besides, you know, I… Well, I'm a dog. I don't think people are used to hearing dogs talk.'

To mollify the lady and to avoid leaving empty-handed, Adelmo Farandola has bought two loaves of bread, two bottles of red wine and some tins of meat, which are now bouncing around in his ripped rucksack.

'If you ask me, that lady didn't believe me,' he grumbles.

'Well, it's possible. What did she say?'

'To go to the carabinieri, I think.'

'And?'

'I didn't go, of course.'

A pause. The steep incline forces them to concentrate on the path.

'I'm not going to the carabinieri. They can come to me if they want to know something.'

'Perhaps the lady will go.'

It's unlikely, thinks Adelmo Farandola. She didn't believe me. She just wanted to go back to bed, back to the warm, back to one of her lovers.

12

'Do you suffer from vertigo?' Adelmo asks the dog that evening.

'Why?' asks the dog, pricking up his ears.

'Nothing. No reason.'

'Where are we going, then? Where are we going?'

The dog starts skipping. Adelmo Farandola already regrets asking him about vertigo.

But by now spring is advancing and soon he'll have to start thinking about moving further up, beyond the reaches of the day trippers who infest the mountain pastures in the summer. So the old man resigns himself and continues.

'Because, you see, in a bit I'll be going into the mountains.'

'Into the mountains? Where do you think we are now?'

'Further up, I mean. Not in the mountains, onto the mountain.'

'And why are you going there?'

'To be left in peace.'

The dog sniffs the air, perplexed. 'It's not peaceful enough here?'

The old man tells him about the day trippers. The dog doesn't seem very worried. To him, day trippers means lots of leftovers.

*

In summer, then, in order to be left properly in peace, Adelmo Farandola takes himself up to an old disused shepherd's hut overlooking a mountain pass between two scree slopes. He scares off the occasional hikers who venture that far by throwing stones at them. The hut is little more than a shelter made of wood and metal sheeting, wobbling above the void at the end of an invisible path used decades ago by smugglers – and only the most desperate or stupid ones. Up there, between the thin metal walls, the man can hardly stretch out full-length to sleep on a bed made of old blankets. During the day, the wind howls through the cracks in the metal and shakes the hut until nightfall, when it suddenly drops.

All this Adelmo Farandola explains to the dog in his own words.

'Whatever makes you happy,' says the dog. 'I gave up trying to understand you early on. But anyway, what will I do? I'll come with you, right?'

'As long as you don't get vertigo.'

'I don't know. I don't think so. Why should the things that cause vertigo bother me? I tend to sniff things.'

'Well, in that case I might take you.'

The shelter is often hidden by the clouds that cling to the steep mountainside and make the rock face slippery. You rarely see the sun up there. It's not unusual for it to snow even in summer. The maps and guides detailing shelters and mountain passes and routes no longer refer to this rugged pass at all, and to get up there you'd have to stumble upon it by chance or by mistake, or by following ancient instructions from the most ancient inhabitants of the villages further down the valley. From below, the hut isn't even visible, because its grey walls match the rock to which it clings. It's just the place to be left in peace, Adelmo Farandola repeats to himself. He's seen how many people find their way to his valley in summer – he's heard the idiotic tourists knocking at his door, asking if there are cheeses for sale, or honey even! Up there in that shelter, barely wider than a man lying down, there is nothing to attract the idiots. Even looking at the view, on the rare days when you can see anything, there's nothing but steep scree slopes, lichen-pocked shards of rock and dry craters where little pools of dark water gather, although they get smaller every year.

'There isn't room for two, though,' Adelmo Farandola says after a while.

'What's that? Have you changed your mind?'

'I'm just saying there isn't room.'

'But I'm a dog, I hardly take up any room! And given how little I've eaten since I've known you, I take up even less now!'

'We'll see.'

'What will we see?'

'I'll think about it. Maybe I'll leave you here.'

'Don't say that.' The dog is getting anxious and lets slip a couple of barks.

Adelmo Farandola chuckles. He hasn't chuckled in years. The dog makes him laugh; he likes teasing him. Perhaps he really will take him to the shepherd's hut and make him sleep on the threshold, balancing tenuously over the abyss, just to amuse himself even more.

He's always liked looking out over precipices and experiencing the sudden feeling of emptying that comes with vertigo. Even more, he likes the way the void opening up before him squeezes his balls. He likes to feel the tug of the vortex of air and of the terrifying panorama rushing down towards the valley floor or stretching away towards other, more distant valleys.

He mostly indulges in this amusement in summer, when he has only to stick his nose out of the hut to find himself hanging over the void. An invisible hand immediately grasps his testicles, while two more pinch his nipples painfully. In that moment he really feels alive and, in a sense, rediscovers parts of himself he'd almost entirely forgotten, remembering them only when an occasional deep itch directs his attention their way. Even then, though, he can't remember what they're for.

If his memory wasn't abandoning him in such a hurry, he would remember similar sensations experienced as a kid in the fields around the farms, where he and other snot-nosed boys used to challenge each other to see who could hold on longest to the wire of the electric fences that ran around the fields of cows. Back then, during those endless, painful duels, the throbbing current drove into his hands like nails, climbed up his arms, jumped into his temples and pressed against his testicles. None of them dared to let go of the wire too soon, for fear that the others would laugh at them for months, throughout those long, boring summer days spent in the most isolated pastures. The last blows of the current felt like punches driven into your teeth, into your eyes. Adelmo Farandola wouldn't give up until he felt that he was close to fainting. Only then would he collapse, stunned, and gaze at his burning, blackened palms.

Back then, he was convinced that he could endure the shocks better than the other boys his age because of the high-voltage cables that passed over the houses down in the village and drove them all mad, men and beasts alike. This conviction gave him strength, so that, with his hand tight around the wire, he really could bear the increasingly violent stinging better than anyone else.

When the crows arrive, the old man is forced to give up one of his blankets to protect the foot. Before dawn, the crows come up in hordes from the distant rubbish heaps of urban landfills down in the main valley and fall greedily on the carcasses as they emerge from the filthy snow. They stay there for hours, squabbling obstinately over pieces of dead meat as if there wasn't enough for everyone.

'Bloody crows!' Adelmo Farandola shouts, hearing them arrive, arrogant and rowdy, before he sees them.

The crows don't even reply. They hop and flap across the black snow, nibbling, pissing each other off, flying away with pieces of meat in their beaks before carelessly dropping them with a thump, laughing like idiots, chasing and insulting each other.

'Crows,' the dog barks with distaste.

For a while, the blanket seems to do its job, but then the creatures work out how to move it by pulling on it with their beaks, so Adelmo Farandola has to pin it to the snow with crampons and weigh it down with stones.

'What're you doing that for?' asks a crow.

'I just am,' says Adelmo Farandola. 'Do what you like with the other animals but leave the man under there alone.'

'Why do you give a shit? It's nothing like a man now.'

'He's still a man.'

'But it's so good! It smells irresistible! Can't you smell it?' asks another crow.

'That smell – what did I tell you?' the dog whispers to the old man. 'They can smell it. It's pretty strong.'

Adelmo Farandola keeps watch on the crows for hours. He lets them peck each other and tear apart the carcasses as they gradually come free from the melting snow – the meat isn't much use to him now that the path to the village is clear again. But he throws stones at them whenever he sees them getting too close to the blanket that hides the foot.

'Hey, you!' they shout at him. 'What the fuck are you doing?'

After a few weeks, the sun has warmed the great heap of snow enough to melt it. Various little rivulets emerge from its base and flow ceaselessly, losing themselves at once in labyrinths carved into the snow and reappearing thunderously further down, where the grassy floor of the pasture turns to scree before plunging towards the main valley. The water's noisy and ice-cold, and it leaps like a living creature and frightens the dog, who barks at it.

'Why are you barking?' asks Adelmo Farandola.

'Well, because... Don't you see it?'

'It's water. What are you barking for?'

'It's water?'

'Yes.'

'You wouldn't think so.'

What a stupid dog, thinks Adelmo Farandola. It's true, though. The water does seem alive. It seems to be fleeing, running far away to safety. One evening, when the crows have gone and it's almost dark, the old man climbs up onto the frozen snowdrift and approaches the blanket. He moves it aside and sees a whole leg.

We're getting there, he thinks. Soon we'll know who on earth he is.

'Anything to see?' asks the dog, as soon as he spots him climbing down.

Adelmo Farandola doesn't answer. He goes back into the cabin and leaves the dog outside until he hears him crying and scratching at the door.

He climbs up onto the heap of snow again the next morning, after driving off the crows. He moves the blanket aside and looks at the naked, twisted foot, the dried-up calf, the withered thigh. A naked leg. Is the rest naked too? Adelmo Farandola wonders. Who knows why he's naked.

He looks more closely, screwing up his eyes. He spots an ant on the remains of a toenail, one of those tiny black ones – the most obstinate kind. He stares at it for a few minutes: it looks around, then wanders off, appearing and disappearing between the brown creases of the toe and the surrounding rubble. He sees it meet another ant, he sees them speak to each other at length, but they're too small and from his height he can't hear what they're saying. He sees them separate after saying goodbye to one another. Two more ants climb up along the calf. Three more appear from behind the calf. Now they get into a line and go off to explore certain cracks on the sole of the foot, certain wounds that the avalanche has carved into the flesh. They wander in and out. He can't tell if they're carrying anything on their backs, fragments of meat perhaps. They would have to be minuscule pieces, just a little taste, just enough to take the edge off the appetite. He puts his face closer to the leg again and at last he notices the smell of the corpse.

'Where are you coming from?' he murmurs as he sees them multiply.

13

As the days pass, even the most obstinate remnants of grubby snow retreat and dissolve into nervous rivulets which plunge down towards the valley below. By this time, the dead man's leg is uncovered as far as the groin and waves in the air, naked and grey. A few scraps of fabric are now visible halfway up the thigh: the remains of a decayed pair of trousers. The force of the avalanche must have stripped that leg and hurled its shoe and sock God knows where. The shrunken leg sways like a young tree trunk. The ants patrol it tirelessly, all day long.

'It makes you think, doesn't it?' says the dog, staring vacantly at the limb.

'What about?'

'I don't know. Life.'

'That thing's not alive.'

'No, exactly, that's why... Oh, what's the use? Forget it,' the dog snorts.

Adelmo Farandola is busy and has stopped answering. The provisions have run out again, so he's gone back to extracting the remnants of bodies that the retreating snow has brought to light: chamois, startled by the sudden snowfall; ibexes, too slow to get away in time; mountain birds, curled up in little feathery balls. He has no desire to go down to the village. There's still well-preserved meat among the debris and if it's not well preserved, never mind, you just cook it thoroughly and make sure you don't breathe in when you put it in your mouth. The dog catches on at last and sticks his tongue out.

'It's better than going hunting, don't you think?' he asks the old man.

'There's enough here to last until summer,' says Adelmo Farandola.

'That way you won't have to eat me.'

Adelmo Farandola stops, straightens up for a moment and stares at the dog.

'Why should I eat you?' he asks.

Look: here's the dead man's abdomen, swollen like that of a drowned man. Here's the chest, staved in by the force of the avalanche. Here are the outstretched hands: first the curled fingers – not all of them, some are missing; others have been snapped in half – then the palms. Then the contorted wrists. Then the forearms.

Here are the shoulders. Part of the head. The gaping mouth. The blackened eye sockets. The face, flattened by the impact. Here's the concave forehead. And, amid the devastation, a few small holes just above the eyes.

'It certainly makes an impression,' says the dog.

'What did you expect?' asks Adelmo Farandola. 'It's the avalanche. Those animals we cooked were in the same state.'

'Do you know him?'

'How should I know? Do you?'

'Hmm. No, I don't think so. Can I give him a little sniff?'

The dog approaches, careful not to put a foot wrong, and sticks out his muzzle, breathing in deeply.

'Well?'

'I couldn't say. I can only smell… well…'

Adelmo Farandola shakes his head and laughs privately to see the dog so unskilled.

'I wonder what those little holes are,' says the dog, stepping back on the grass.

He's seen the little punctures on the forehead too – not the sort of wound you get from an avalanche. An avalanche either skins you and crushes you or it leaves you intact. There are no half-measures; little holes and punctures aren't part of the deal.

After a while, the two of them come back to look at the emerging body. Together, they stare at the shattered face and the holes in the forehead.

'Actually, those could be bullet holes,' says the dog.

Adelmo Farandola shrugs his shoulders.

'Could be all sorts.'

'The more I look at this guy, the more he reminds me of that nice ranger who came to see us in the autumn. Look at the clothes. That's his uniform, isn't it?'

The clothes are sparse rags, drenched in water and mud. The avalanche has shredded them, ripped out their seams and deformed them. It's impossible to say if they once constituted a uniform, but the dog insists, supporting his argument with petulant barks, which the old man is forced to counter with haphazard kicks.

Ranger or no ranger, Adelmo Farandola decides one morning that he should remove the cadaver from the remains of the snowdrift and hide it where no one will be able to find it. For once, he is able to grasp the situation immediately and see the matter quite clearly, because this morning he awoke from a night crowded with dreams in which the unknown man with the forehead full of holes came and stood next to him and followed him everywhere, like a dog.

'Go on, shoo,' Adelmo Farandola had muttered, trying to get away from it, but the agile corpse had followed him, appearing suddenly at his side, like a dog. It had been half-naked, its skin black, its face caved in, with the holes clearly visible, and there had been columns of ants swarming all over its limbs.

'What's this? What are we doing?' asks the dog, when he realizes that Adelmo Farandola is getting ready for some unusual activity.

'Go on, shoo,' the old man answers, because this morning the dog reminds him too much of the corpse that dogged his footsteps all night long.

'Oh, very polite!' barks the dog, and takes himself off, temporarily offended.

Adelmo Farandola takes an old spade from the stable and a stout rope and makes for the remains of the avalanche. He stopped bothering to protect the dead body with the blanket some time ago and the crows, kestrels, choughs and buzzards have started arriving before dawn to take advantage of this fact. The earliest risers are already on the corpse, pecking away avidly. The bolder ones challenge them, attacking with their beaks, constantly distracting them, forcing them to interrupt their meal and leave their places to chase off the interlopers. The shy ones and the late arrivals circle overhead, waiting for the others to tire, only risking the occasional dive into the heaving mass of feathers. Further off, two gaunt foxes wait, resigned to making do with the bones.

Adelmo Farandola chases them all away with shouts and stones, then clambers up what little snow and ice remains of the heap. He bends over the dead body, which the birds have hollowed out and riddled with holes. The animals' tireless work has moved the carcass; now, with its limbs spreadeagled, it seems about to take flight, or to hurl itself into an abyss.

'There you are,' murmurs Adelmo Farandola.

Once he has inexpertly freed the corpse from the surrounding detritus with the spade, he ties it around his shoulders, passing the rope under its armpits. He climbs out of the puddle that has formed around him and back down the heap, dragging the body out with him. Meanwhile the birds, who have grown reckless, flap ever closer, coming at him from all sides, complaining and brushing him with their wings and their beaks.

Today he doesn't think it looks like the ranger any more. It doesn't look like anyone, not a soul. It's more like the shapeless remnant of a tree growing high up a mountain, one of those trees that survive among the scree slopes thanks to their mysterious root systems and that grow painfully twisted and deformed by the wind.

'Where are you taking our friend?' asks the dog, who has already forgotten his resentment.

'Away from here.'

'I can see that. But where?'

'None of your business.'

'To the shepherd's hut?'

'Don't talk nonsense.'

Adelmo Farandola is concentrating on a thought. He repeats it to himself endlessly, so as not to forget it. It seems like a good plan, or perhaps the only possible one. He will drag the corpse to the old manganese mine and shove it into the depths of the earth, as far down as he can. No one will find it there; even the birds won't be able to reach it. The worms alone will taste its flesh and its bones. The great scaly worms whose ancestors transformed themselves into rock, and that surely still inhabit the depths of the mountain, will make it disappear, bite by bite.

'Where the fuck are you going? What the fuck are you doing?' scream the crows, the least willing to leave him in peace.

But Adelmo Farandola doesn't reply. Step by step, he climbs the steep paths that lead to the old mine, dislodging loose stones and, when the ascent becomes too difficult, clutching at lonely tufts of mountain pine.

The dog follows him. He's gone back to playing the affectionate companion. He understands that this isn't the moment for conversation and keeps quiet. He uses the time to sniff everything and sneeze with happiness.

'Why are you doing this? Hadn't we agreed to tell someone?' the dog says eventually.

'No, we mustn't tell anyone,' says Adelmo Farandola,

who is sitting down on the slope, preparing to face the final gruelling stretch.

'But we went down into the village to tell someone about it just last week!'

'Really?'

'Yes! You told the lady in the shop.'

'I don't think so.'

'And she told you to tell the carabinieri.'

'And did I?'

'No, you didn't.'

'Good. And did the lady believe me?'

'I doubt it. I think she thought you were off your rocker.'

'Perfect. So we hide it and that's that.'

A few of the most obstinate birds are still hanging around nearby.

'What's this moron doing?' they ask the dog. 'Where's he taking it?'

'What's it to you?' barks the dog.

'Hey, moron! We're talking to you!' the birds squawk at the dog, who snaps at the air to scare them off.

'Look, you know as much as I do,' he grumbles at last. 'Far away from you, that's for sure. Far away from everyone.'

'What bullshit.'

'It's what they call a proper burial.'

'What a waste! He's just giving it to the animals that live underground.'

'That's how it is. Now kindly clear off.'

'Fuck you, slave.'

Adelmo Farandola keeps quiet. The more he thinks about it, the more he seems to remember being the one who fired the round that hit the man he's dragging behind him right between the eyes. Slowly, as he excavates his memory – his pathetic excuse for a memory, which confuses everything – he manages to find a few fragments of recollection. He doesn't know if they're real memories or the fake memories you create when you suddenly realize you're living through a situation you've already experienced, and you look around, dazed, not understanding where and when this moment has happened before, and the uncertainty is so vivid that it almost takes your breath away. Adelmo Farandola doesn't know if this memory really has emerged from the vast confusion in his head or if he's invented it himself, after dwelling on it so much over the last few days; or if he's confused one of his many dreams with a real memory; or if he's dreaming even now, a long, tiresome, irritating dream that will leave him in a bad mood all morning, even after he's forgotten it. But yes, it's true that somewhere inside his head there's this little memory, which sometimes seems to grow quite clear, of picking up the shotgun and firing. It's something he's done hundreds of times, that's for sure. But he can't say whether he was deliberately trying to hit the tattered creature he is now dragging behind him over the stones or whether it was a bloody accident.

'If in doubt, better get it out of the way,' he says to the dog.

'Please yourself,' the dog replies. 'But wouldn't it have been better to bury it further down?'

'It's not safe. I want to hide it properly.'

'I see.'

'And I know where.'

14

Everything seems to be falling into place in the laborious reconstruction Adelmo Farandola is piecing together in his mind. He can see it, the fatal moment: higher up the mountain where the scree slopes are, at the foot of the first overhanging cliffs, where he sometimes goes in search of meat. The ranger had been tracking him for a while and surprised him while he was shooting at an ibex or a chamois. And there's the gunshot. He thinks he can still hear it echoing. The ranger reached him, called to him, ordered him to stop, to put down the gun – somewhere between the walls of his head, a shout is still reverberating, 'Stop!' or something like that, a shrill 'Stop!' pronounced with a sort of malignant cheerfulness. Adelmo Farandola turned, but didn't put down the gun. He doesn't like other people telling him what to do. He would never have put down the gun. Quite the opposite: he'd have clutched it even more tightly, he'd have aimed it towards that high-pitched 'Stop!' as a challenge, to see if the other man would have the courage to say it again – 'Stop!' in a voice so high-pitched that it sounded almost feminine. What do you mean, 'Stop', little boy? Who are you telling to stop, you idiot? This whole valley is mine, all of it, from here to there. Who are you telling to stop? This is my land. Everything that moves among these rocks is mine. These are things that might have been said. Adelmo Farandola repeats them to himself out loud, and he thinks that yes, he might well have said just that, those exact words. Then the gunshot, the discharge of bullets. The ranger crumpling, not understanding. His eyes, begging the old man to call someone, not to leave him there. Instead, Adelmo Farandola hurries back to the cabin, his heart pounding, and shuts himself inside and manages to forget it all, one page at a time, one breath at a time, until that day shrinks to become a day like any other, long and slow and uniform. Then the turning of the season, the first snowfall, then the December avalanches, which always come crashing down on either side of the cabin. One of them brought the ranger's body with it and held it in its womb for all of winter and part of spring, nurturing it coldly and silently before melting and leaving it behind, flattened by the pressure and the impact, ready for the crows.

'That's how it happened,' he says to the dog.

'But do you remember it?'

'No need. That's how it happened.'

'Hang on, though, where was I? I would have noticed, wouldn't I?'

'You go wandering off on your own sometimes. You hare off, chasing a scent, without telling me anything. It must have been one of those times. They can last hours.'

'I...' the dog begins, then breaks off, because it's true, he does go haring off on his own when a trail of foul smells seduces him, making him forget everything else, making him feel completely alive and wild, turning him into a predator, master of life and death.

'That's how it happened,' Adelmo Farandola repeats. 'No word of a lie. I killed this one myself.'

With a mountain dweller's ferocious patience, Adelmo Farandola drags the corpse as far as the old mine where, as a young man, he hid from the men in greatcoats and their gunfire. Driven by a vague recollection, he hunts around among the crumbling rocks and the stony ground. A few obstinate bushes of dwarf juniper, rhododendron and mountain pine have grown in a senseless tangle by the various entrances to the mine. They alone can survive on the arid mountain heath. That's good, Adelmo Farandola says to himself. These shrubs, permanently on the point of dying, will hide the tunnel mouths from even the most careful eye.

He measures the openings and discounts any that are too large and easy. He chooses one that is almost invisible, being narrow and partially obstructed by landslide debris. The old man moves the rocks patiently, letting them crash down into the valley, not worrying where they end up. After a few hours' work, he's created three or four metres of space inside the tunnel. He ventures inside on all fours. The tunnel narrows almost immediately and from there he advances on elbows and knees through the icy black slime.

Outside, the dog keeps his eyes on the man's feet.

'How's it looking?' he asks. 'Is there room for our man in there?'

Adelmo Farandola doesn't reply. He advances further, scraping against the loose soil on the narrow tunnel walls. He carves himself out a passage and proceeds, wheezing.

'Well, when he gets like this...' the dog mutters to himself, outside, his ears pricked up, his eyes raised to heaven.

After almost an hour, the old man's feet emerge, then his backside, like a breech birth.

'Well?' says the dog, once the entire man has appeared. 'I was starting to worry.'

'There's more soil I need to bring out.'

'Ah. What with?'

Adelmo Farandola takes off his jacket, ties off the arms and turns it over to give it the shape of a bag.

'It'll take days,' sighs the dog.

For three days, Adelmo Farandola comes and goes from the tunnel, extracting mud and debris, which he pours away down a gorge. No one will notice the fresh soil – at this time of year everything's shifting and subsiding. His exhaustion and the biting air make him gasp like a dying man. When he's out in the open, the dog watches his every movement with resignation, but he stays by the corpse, refusing to budge, and has lost any desire to speak.

Finally, Adelmo Farandola decides that he's cleared a sufficient stretch of tunnel. He takes the corpse, hauls it as far as the opening and drags it inside by the ankles.

'You're coming back, right?' whispers the dog.

Where the tunnel narrows so much that there's only room for a single body, Adelmo Farandola slithers over the corpse and starts working from the other end, pushing it by the shoulders.

'Hey, careful!' the corpse complains.

'Sorry,' Adelmo Farandola mutters.

It's still lovely inside, like when he was young – that's one thing he really does remember. The atmosphere isn't exactly welcoming, but it provides a pleasant sense of protection. There's good company, too, and food, if you search well with your hands. Adelmo Farandola relaxes his muscles one by one and slips into a long sleep.

The dog is unhappy. He howls by the mouth of the tunnel, scratches disconsolately at the ground and tries to crawl inside. But Adelmo Farandola shoos him away from inside, threatens to shoot him, swears at him and disowns him.

'But it's me, old friend! It's me!' the dog implores.

'Go away. No one wants you. Who are you? Who are you?'

'It's me! Come on, that's enough. This isn't fun.'

'I should have eaten you on the first day.'

'You're joking, right?'

'Should have eaten you and sucked your bones one by one, damned dog.'

The dog says nothing and trembles.

'Go! Go away or they'll find me!'

'No! I'll come and stay by your side! I'll be good. I'll be as quiet as a mouse. We'll keep each other warm… Corpses don't stay warm, but I will!'

'Go away or I'll shoot you.'

'You need me, I know it.'

'Balls.'

'Don't abandon me, please.'

Adelmo Farandola says nothing and, with his silence, hopes to forget the dog and be forgotten by him. The dog curls up on the threshold silently and with immense sadness, trying to content himself with the smell of his human friend as it rises like invisible smoke from the tunnel, mixed with the pungently sweet smell of the dead man.

'Are you still there?' Adelmo Farandola barks after a while, from the depths of the tunnel, his voice unrecognizable.

'No,' the dog whispers.

That bloody stray, thinks Adelmo Farandola. As soon as they arrive, he'll start jumping for joy, like he did with me on the first day. That is – I imagine he was like that on the first day, because I don't remember it very well. Actually I don't remember it at all. But I know what he's like because he's been getting under my feet for as long as I can remember. He's like that with everyone.

Then again, that's dogs for you. They sell themselves for a piece of bread. They stick to you for life. You put them outside so they can do their business and they stay there, on the doorstep, and do it all over themselves because you're not there and they won't take a single step without you. That's dogs for you.

He'll start wagging his tail as soon as they put out a hand to pat him. He'll roll over and beg for more, that disgrace to the male sex. And if they say, 'There's a good boy, now where is Adelmo Farandola?' he'll tell them straight away. 'In there, my dear, dear friends, inside the tunnel of an old mine, wedged inside the rock like a suppository in an arsehole.' 'Really? Thanks so much. What a good boy.' 'Not at all, friends. I'll take you there, if you like. By the way, what's for dinner?'

That's what he'll do, the mongrel.

He's never liked dogs.

That's what he'll do.

'Well...' whispers the dead man next to him.

'Well what?'

'It would be a real pain if they found us.'

'Exactly.'

'And I'm not thinking about myself here. These days I... Well, I'm mostly worried for you.'

Adelmo Farandola listens and keeps quiet. In the cold, damp darkness of the tunnel, his new fellow fugitive creaks and exhales.

'Excuse me,' he says.

'Don't mention it,' says Adelmo Farandola. Meanwhile he's thinking about what to do with the dog.

'They haven't arrived yet,' says the dead man. 'You'd still have time.'

Outside, the dog has gone back to whining and barking impatiently. It's stopped talking and is acting like a dog – just a normal dog – to move its old companion to pity.

'What a bore,' sighs the dead man.

15

When he can no longer hear barking, Adelmo Farandola crawls out of the tunnel. The night is illuminated by a wan gibbous moon. The dog is sleeping. As it sleeps, it trembles, stirring its paws silently. It doesn't seem to notice the old man's arrival. Adelmo Farandola looks around him, trying to find something to hit it with.

As he brings the stone down on the dog's skull, the old man realizes it was only feigning sleep, hoping to prolong this moment of closeness with its friend as much as possible and prevent the rift between them from growing wider. It's been as good as gold: it's waited obligingly for him to decide what to do and choose a big enough stone. Then, a second before the stone comes crashing down, the dog half-opens an eye and lets slip a brief whine, full of love. The dog knows instinctively that the guilt for having cut off that whine won't survive long in Adelmo Farandola's ransacked mind, but it contents itself with the knowledge that, for a while, its murderer will feel a confused mixture of regret and guilt. That, perhaps, is enough.

'So, how did it go?' the dead man asks when Adelmo Farandola crawls backwards down the tunnel and slides into place next to him a few hours later.

The old man doesn't reply.

'Did you hide it?'

In the dark, Adelmo Farandola nods.

'They won't find it, will they?'

'No.'

'Those people search everywhere.'

'I buried it a long way away. They won't see it. And even if they see it, they can't trace it back to us.'

'Good. Excellent. Now we can relax.'

'Exactly.'

'Goodnight, my dear,' says the dead man, before falling silent once more.

Sunk in his tunnel, the old man hears a voice calling him by name: 'Adelmo! Adelmo!' He doesn't know who it can be, but the voice has something unusually familiar about it.

'Adelmo, sodding Christ almighty, Adelmo!'

The voice bounces between the valley walls, between moraine and rockfall, between overhanging cliffs and scree slopes, and finds its way to him even at the bottom of his tunnel, coming in bursts and waves, multiplied by the echo.

'Who's that now?' grumbles the corpse.

'I don't know.'

'I hope this shithole of a tunnel has another exit.'

'No, no. That's what's so good about it.'

'Ah. Brilliant idea, sticking us in here.'

The voice from the valley seems to be approaching, getting closer with each shout, and then suddenly it retreats and moves off in another direction.

'They won't find us,' says Adelmo Farandola.

'And what if they find the dog?'

'What dog?'

'The one that... Oh, forget it.'

'Adelmo! Adelmo!' The word keeps echoing, on and on for hours.

Annoyed, Adelmo Farandola decides to take a look outside and see who's searching for him. He shuffles on his stomach as far as the opening and comes to the surface covered in sand and soil. He pokes his nose outside, then his whole head. The light of the overcast day blinds him and burns his eyes. Once he's got used to the brightness, his throbbing eyes make out a helicopter on the ground further down the mountain, right in the middle of his valley.

'There they are,' he says under his breath.

From the bottom of the tunnel, the corpse asks him questions.

Quiet, quiet, thinks Adelmo Farandola. Quiet, or they'll hear us. He forces himself to look more closely in the direction of the helicopter. He thinks he can make out two pairs of men walking around the valley. Two of them have stopped in front of the cabin, which, from above, looks like a heap of stones, hardly more ordered than the others around it. That's where the shouting is coming from. A man, an old man, his voice amplified by a loudspeaker, says his name three more times, coughing, before his voice gives out and he falls silent. The other man stands by his side.

The second pair are climbing the narrow gully that leads up to his summer shelter. What idiots, Adelmo Farandola thinks smugly, a half-smile on his face. Who do they think I am? He follows them with eyes that are still keen, in spite of his age. They're a long way off, on completely the wrong track, and they won't ever find him. He seeks refuge in the shade of his tunnel and rests his burning eyes. From there, indifferent to everything around him, he slides back into the depths.

'See anything?' asks the corpse.

'Four idiots.'

'The world's full of them.'

Outside, the amplified voice of the old man starts up again.

'Adelmo! Adelmino!'

Is my name really Adelmo? Adelmo Farandola wonders. Is it really me they're looking for?

'Adelmo, listen! It's Armando!'

Armando? Who could that be? Adelmo Farandola wonders.

'Armando, Adelmo! Your brother Armando! Can you hear me?'

A brother. Rubbish. He remembers having a brother, yes, and perhaps he was called Armando too, but he was much younger, barely more than a boy – not a hoarse old man.

'Sodding Christ almighty, Adelmo, where are you?'

His little brother used to say 'sodding Christ almighty' like that – and that was when he was being polite, laughs Adelmo Farandola. Funny, these little coincidences.

'Adelmo! Adelmino! Look, what else can I say? Oh, right. Adelmino, I'm passing you over to someone you know well.'

A pause, a confusion of randomly amplified voices, interference, crackling.

I don't know anyone, Adelmo Farandola is thinking, and I'm quite happy that way.

'Adelmo!' shouts a young man's voice, making him jump. 'Adelmo, my friend!'

Adelmo Farandola listens.

'Do you recognize me? It's Mutolo, Severino Mutolo, the ranger. Adelmo, if you can hear me... We've been looking for you for a while now, you know. We're coming to find you. Stay calm! Hold on! We won't leave you.'

Something is stirring confusedly in Adelmo Farandola's head.

The second voice sounds familiar and distant at the same time, like a voice he's listened to recently, but distractedly and with growing boredom.

'It's me, Severino Mutolo, the ranger. Do you remember?'

What can there be to remember? Yes – wait – a uniform, something like that. A uniformed busybody who came to interrogate him every day.

'At least let us see you, Adelmo! If you can't get down, can you give us a sign? Anything, just so we can work out where you are. Don't strain yourself, though. Anything will do, even a stone – yes, one of your stones! You need looking after! Your brother here, Mr Armando, will take care of everything! He loves you, you know. Adelmo, can you hear me?'

More thought fragments return and come together in Adelmo Farandola's chaotic mind. Not troubling to listen further, he slides back towards the corpse.

'So, in that case, who are you?' he whispers in the corpse's ear.

'Oh, *me*. Who *was* I, you mean?'

'Yes, that's what I mean.'

'Well, what does it matter now?'

'You're not the one out there talking?'

'That's a very strange sort of question.'

'You're not him, are you?'

'Well, no. At least, I shouldn't think so.'

Adelmo Farandola hesitates, thinking. His face darkens. He forces himself to put his ideas in order, like when he's on the verge of sleep, climbing backwards through a web of thoughts and associations to find the end of the thread, as his consciousness twitches a few last times before falling asleep.

'How did we end up down here again?'

'You're asking me? You brought me here.'

'Why?'

'How should I know? You found me down there in a snowdrift, and instead of calling someone, you waited until I started to rot and then hid me in here. Much good may it do you.'

'Why did I do that?'

'Well, I don't know! You were there and there was this dog, but then –'

'What dog?'

'Anyway, from what I remember, you were convinced that you'd killed me.'

'And I didn't?'

'No, of course you didn't! And if I ever said that you did, or agreed that it all happened like that, it's because I get a bit confused about things too – but after all, I'm dead and that gives me a good excuse, doesn't it?'

'I didn't kill you.'

'No, no, no. What nonsense.'

'So who are you, then?'

'I don't know. I don't remember,' the corpse mimics him.

The tunnel has suddenly become very cold. Outside the voices have grown distant. Perhaps they're going away, thinks Adelmo Farandola. Perhaps they've given up and they're going away. He doesn't know whether to be pleased or disappointed. He hears the rumble of the helicopter engine starting up, as it rises to explore the smaller valleys and crevices for a while before flying away.

'I know what you're thinking right now,' whispers the corpse, 'but you're not going to leave me here alone. Don't even try it.'

'But who are you?' Adelmo Farandola asks the corpse again, a little later. There are no more sounds from outside, no more voices – but it's a temporary silence. It sounds like they're waiting for more helicopters to carry out even more thorough searches, with dogs and walkie-talkies and all the rest.

'Does it really matter who I am?'

'Yes, to me. Did I kill you?'

'Could be. But no, I don't think so. It doesn't seem likely. I just remember being struck on the head,' the dead man murmurs. 'A short stabbing feeling here, between the eyes. Pain I can't even describe. But it didn't last long, only a moment. I really don't know if it was you. I stayed on my feet, I remember that quite clearly. Like a tree. I died on my feet – an enviable death. It took an avalanche to get me lying down. Are you even listening to me?'

Adelmo Farandola worms himself even deeper into the soil, to savour the cold.

'No, clearly you're not listening to me,' sighs the dead man, like a wife.

Adelmo Farandola stretches a hand along the surface of the rock surrounding him. He's detected a rapid scampering and he knows it must be one of the little blind, translucent arthropods that live underground: a mite, a beetle, a little spider. He wonders for a moment if they're really edible – but the lack of any discernible flavour makes him forget his anxiety straight away.

'Must you chew like that?' the dead man asks.

Adelmo Farandola doesn't answer.

'Did I ever tell you about the power cables?' he says instead, after a pause.

The corpse sighs. 'Yes, more than once.'

'Because if I have gone mad it's because of those cables.'

'You've already told me that too.'

'They passed right over our heads and I heard them buzzing for years when I was a boy.'

'You don't say.'

'We all went mad, in my village. Men and beasts. Everyone.'

Adelmo Farandola means: when the cables buzzed more loudly, we used to fly at each other's throats, sons at their mothers, fathers at their sons, humans at inanimate objects, animals at humans. A few people copped it that way, back then, and not because they went looking for a fight or anything like that, but because of that buzzing, which concentrated our darkest thoughts and brought them to the surface, making them stronger and more definite. And, Adelmo Farandola would like to say, I still hear those cables, even if I don't see them overhead any more. I still hear them inside, and if I've gone mad it's just because of that never-ending buzzing.

That's what he would like to say. But the dead man next to him pretends not to care.

Translator's Note

The story you have just read appears to have two main characters: an old man and a dog. But as the novel unfolds, the mountain landscape almost becomes a third protagonist. It is ever-present, impassive, implacable, beautiful and threatening. Adelmo Farandola is stubbornly determined to survive in this most inhospitable of settings. He and the mountain suit one another – or better, they deserve one another.

This strong sense of place was one of the hardest things to translate. The English language is well suited to describing English geography; it struggles a bit with the scale of the Alps. We have only one word for avalanche, while Italian has two. We have a few synonyms for valley, but it's hard to capture the precise nuances of *vallone*, *vallata* and *conca*. The very first sentence of the Italian novel contains the words *baita* and *malga*, which immediately let the Italian reader know that we're in the Alps. The English equivalents are less precise, so I can only hope that you came prepared with a vivid imagination, well stocked with Alpine scenery, to compensate for any loss of richness in the translation.

This story is itself rather mountainous: it's dark and sharp and uncomfortable in places, but sometimes, at the end of a long climb, you glimpse something unexpectedly beautiful. The story is also very funny. It is often said that humour is the hardest thing to translate, but the characters in this novel are so alive, and so instantly recognizable in their absurdities, delusions and awkwardnesses, that they jumped straight off the Italian page and started bickering on the English one with a minimum of fuss. Claudio Morandini's novel has been a pleasure to translate and remains as fascinating on the hundredth close rereading as it was when I first explored it. My particular thanks go to the author for his kindness and willingness to answer my many questions about the text.

I worked on this story of bitter Alpine harshness from the comfort of an idyllic mill in the Pyrenees, thanks to the extraordinary generosity of Martha Stevns. In creating the Peirene Stevns Translation Prize, she and Peirene Press have provided an unparalleled opportunity for young translators to see their work in print. I am incredibly grateful to them and I look forward to reading many more translations by future prizewinners! My thanks also to Jennifer Higgins, who oversaw this translation from its very earliest stages, to Gesche Ipsen, whose unerring editorial judgement shaped it into the book you are now reading, and to all my friends, relations and godparents who read chapters of the work in progress and weighed in on important questions about dog ears, the effect of vertigo on the testicles and the correct spelling of plateaus.

2020

Peirene STEVNS TRANSLATION PRIZE

The Peirene Stevns Translation Prize was launched in 2018 to support up-and-coming translators.

Open to all translators without a published novel, this prize looks not only to award great translation but also to offer new ways of entry into the world of professional translation. The winner receives a £3,000 commission to translate a text selected by Peirene Press, the opportunity to spend two months at a retreat in the Pyrenees and a dedicated one-on-one mentorship throughout the translation process.

The Peirene Stevns Prize focuses on a different language each year and is open for submissions from October to January.

With thanks to Martha Stevns, without whom this prize would not be possible.

Peirene is proud to support
Women for Refugee Women.

Women for Refugee Women is a UK-based charity that supports women who are seeking asylum and challenges the injustices they experience. The charity runs a range of activities for refugee women, including English classes, drama and writing workshops, with the aim of empowering them to tell their own stories. Women for Refugee Women also advocates for a fairer asylum process and works towards a world in which all women who cross borders have the right to liberty, safety and dignity.